# FRIENDS MAKE
## THE DIFFERENCE

Books in the Forever Friends series

# FRIENDS MAKE THE DIFFERENCE

## Lynn Craig

**THOMAS NELSON PUBLISHERS**
Nashville • Atlanta • London • Vancouver

Published in Nashville, Tennessee, by Thomas Nelson, Inc.,
Publishers, and distributed in Canada by Word
Communications, Ltd., Richmond, British Columbia.

**Library of Congress Cataloging-in-Publication Data**

Craig, Lynn.
    Friends make the difference / Lynn Craig.
       p.   cm. — (Forever friends series : bk. 2)
    Summary: Fourteen-year-old Katelyn and her friends, in
an attempt to have fun and provide community service at
the same time, successfully launch the Forever Friends
club.
    ISBN 0-8407-9240-9 (pbk.)
    [1. Clubs—Fiction.  2. Diaries—Fiction.  3. Friendship—
Fiction.  4. Christian life—Fiction.]  I. Title.  II. Series:
Craig, Lynn. Forever friends series : bk. 2.
PZ7.C84426Fr   1994
[Fic]—dc20                             94–2938
                                                CIP
                                                  AC

Printed in the United States of America.
1 2 3 4 5 6 — 99 98 97 96 95 94

*To*

Gillian and Laurel Ryan

# *Chapter One*

# Missing Pieces

**Wednesday**
**9 P.M.**

"That's her! There she is! That's her!"

And that, dear Journal, is how I nearly caused an accident at the corner of 4th and Elm this morning. Aunt Beverly and I were driving to The Wonderful Life Shop and we were both a little sleepy. My enthusiasm—which I *know* I must learn to curb—gave extra volume to my words and that startled Aunt Beverly, who immediately slammed on the brakes of her Roadmaster station wagon, which caused a chain reaction and lots of squealing brakes behind us, which in turn captured the attention of several drivers going the other direction, who also slammed on their brakes. Fortunately, no cars collided.

"Who?" said Aunt Beverly as she hit the brakes.

"The girl who looks like Emily!" I shouted.

"Who's Emily?" said Aunt Beverly, still puzzled, but at that point significantly more concerned about the traffic than about what I was saying.

I realized of course that I hadn't told Aunt Beverly the entire story, so I just said, "I'll tell you when we get to the shop." Aunt Beverly really was very kind. She didn't seem too exasperated as she pulled the car behind the shop and into her parking space.

Once inside, we finished our "opening routine"—unlocking the front door, turning the sign in the front window over so that it read "Open" instead of "Closed." I swept off the front porch and cleaned the glass door of a few stray fingerprints while Aunt Beverly took cash from the safe in the back room and opened the cash register. We then both got busy with our feather dusters, making sure that all of the beautiful things in the shop were sparkling and, as Aunt Beverly says, "ready for customer muster." Aunt Beverly has such a way with words . . . I think probably she should be a novelist, too. I can hardly wait until I truly *am* one.

While we were dusting, I told Aunt Beverly about the tintype of a girl named Emily at the base of the fountain in a little courtyard right next to the park that is next to the high school, and how

I had gone to this courtyard to eat lunch during the first few weeks since we moved to Collinsville. I also told her about seeing a girl at the Wilsons' swimming party a few weeks ago who looked just like the girl in the tintype photo, and about how I was wondering what the connection might be.

"Maybe it's the same girl?" Aunt Beverly said with a question in her voice.

"Don't think so," I replied. "The plaque on the base of the fountain says, 'In memory of Emily, 1922–1940.'"

"Then it's probably *not* the same girl," laughed Aunt Beverly. "So I take it that you think you spotted the girl you saw at the party while we were causing a near traffic mishap a few minutes ago?"

"Exactly. She was coming out of McGreggor's and she went around the corner." I silently wished that I had asked Aunt Beverly to follow her.

"Well, maybe you'll see her again. Next time, however—" Aunt Beverly said.

Before she could complete her sentence—which I could have completed for her anyway—a customer came in the door, jangling the bells loudly. "Anybody home?" he called.

It was none other than Mr. Wonderful Customer himself, Clark Weaver.

"Hi, Mr. Weaver," I said in what Dad calls my "perky voice."

"Hello, Katelyn," said Mr. Clark Weaver, helping himself to a complimentary cup of coffee that Aunt Beverly had just finished brewing. "Is your aunt here?"

"Sure am," said Aunt Beverly. *How did she put on fresh lipstick that fast?* I wondered.

"I came in early to see if we have any furniture to move today," he said, giving her his usual giant-sized grin—this time with the bonus of a wink.

"Actually, you do," said Aunt Beverly. "That is, of course, if you like the table and chairs I have in the back room. I have them on consignment from another shop, so if you don't like what you see— no problem. I can return them without question."

"Let's see what you found," said Mr. Clark Weaver, picking up one of the new titles on the table by the front door as he followed Aunt Beverly into the back of the store. I stayed out front, continuing to dust all the beautiful things that Aunt Beverly has in her shop.

I never get tired of looking at the things in the shop. All the beautiful books, especially the big photo books that Aunt Beverly calls "coffee-table books." And the gift items—I especially like the new little porcelain animals that just came in. They look like real forest animals and birds—only smaller. Like something straight out of the Beatrix Potter series—great little books, in my opinion, for people of all ages, even teen-agers! And just this past week, Aunt Beverly received a shipment of

4

embroidered napkins and tablecloths from China. They are incredibly beautiful. I don't know how Aunt Beverly can afford to sell them for so little money.

Anyway . . . while I was dusting away and taking out withered blooms from the flower arrangements in the vases scattered throughout the shop . . . I could still hear most of what Aunt Beverly and Mr. Clark Weaver were saying.

"Perfect," said Mr. Clark Weaver. "I could have hunted for weeks and never found something like that."

"Are you sure the chairs are comfortable to you? That's the most important thing about dining chairs. So many of them look great but are terribly uncomfortable."

"Positive. A person sitting in one of these chairs could linger over dessert and coffee for a long time," he said. "Isn't it a little odd that there are only five chairs?"

"Oh, there really are six," said Aunt Beverly. "I'm sorry I didn't think to tell you. One of the chairs needed a little repair work. My brother took it down to the store—Stone's Hardware—to fix it."

"Great," said Mr. Clark Weaver. "How much do I owe you?"

"Only three hundred fifty," said Aunt Beverly, and then quickly added, "I hope that isn't too much."

"It's a steal," said Mr. Clark Weaver. "Antiques are expensive, but I couldn't even get a new set as nice as that for that amount. Does that include your fee, or should I add more to the check?"

By this time the two of them had returned to the front of the store and Mr. Clark Weaver was busy writing in his checkbook.

"No fee for me," said Aunt Beverly. "This is a fun project for me, not a job."

"But I insist," said Mr. Clark Weaver. He was as serious as I've ever heard him.

"No way," said Aunt Beverly, folding her arms and looking very stubborn. "If you insist, then I'll cease and desist. No more decorating suggestions."

"Is that your absolutely *final* decision?" asked Mr. Clark Weaver.

"Absolutely," said Aunt Beverly. "You don't know what a challenge it is to try to turn a genuine bachelor's pad into a respectable house in central Collinsville." This time it was Aunt Beverly who had the grin on her face.

"Glad to provide a challenge," said Mr. Clark Weaver. "Be sure to ring up this book. I'll pay cash for it. And also—a pound of that Raspberry Cream decaffeinated coffee."

"It's delicious," said Aunt Beverly as she turned to the cannisters behind her and scooped out a pound of the coffee he had requested. A faint whiff of raspberry filled the air. I don't drink coffee, but

6

I was sure glad Aunt Beverly brewed a pot of that particular flavor for the customers today. I love the smell.

And then—f-i-n-a-l-l-y, in my opinion—I heard the words I've been waiting to hear for weeks from the lips of Mr. Clark Weaver. "I'd like to buy you dinner, Beverly. Will you at least share a meal of appreciation with me?"

"That I'll do," said Aunt Beverly as she put his purchases in a little sack and gave him his change. I had been holding my breath in fear that she'd say no. After all, his invitation still sounded a bit like payment to me.

"I'll phone you about day, time, and place," he said. "For now, I'd better go find Jon and see if we can move this furniture over the lunch hour." As he turned to walk out the front door, he added with a grin, "I think I know just where to find him—in front of the closest mirror. We're both trying to get used to the New Look."

With that, he left, and Aunt Beverly and I burst into giggles. "Dinner?" I teased. "I hope it's someplace magnificent. Maybe he'll take you to the Manor House."

"Probably to Mexico Pete's," she said with a grimace.

"No," I said. "That sounded like a real-date invitation to me."

"Mexico Pete's is real," she laughed.

"Not what I had in mind," I said.

"The New Look," said Aunt Beverly, conveniently changing subjects. "Do you think Jon is really pleased?"

"He'd better be," I said. Two customers came into the shop so I said quickly, "I'll restock the candies and teas."

While I worked, I thought of nothing but Jon Weaver. Lucky for me I didn't get the caramels mixed up with the peppermints.

The transformation of Jon last week was one of the most amazing things I have ever seen.

Let's see . . . it started on Tuesday.

It really is difficult for me to keep my days straight when I don't write in you, dear Journal, every day or so. But more of my excuse about that later.

Aunt Beverly and I met Jon at nine o'clock on Tuesday morning. Aunt Beverly wanted to get an idea about his wardrobe. I could tell that Jon had made a special effort to have his room picked up and clean. How did I know? Well, magazine edges were sticking out of one drawer, and I could see a stack of papers peeking out behind the nightstand. *At least he tried!* I thought.

He and Aunt Beverly surveyed the closet for a few minutes, talking the entire time about what colors Jon liked and what styles he found the most comfortable to wear. I was really surprised to hear Jon say, "I'd like to dress more like my dad."

"Well, why don't you?" Aunt Beverly asked.

"Most of my clothes come from my Grandmother Turner," he said. "After Mom died, Grandmother said to Dad that she didn't trust a bachelor to keep her grandson looking respectable . . . so every month or so, I get a little packet from Grandmother Turner with new clothes in them. She always calls first to see what sizes I'm wearing."

"So it's Grandmother Turner who sends you the button-down shirts?" I said. Things were suddenly making sense. I hadn't been able to understand Jon's wardrobe choices, especially since his father had such a sandals-and-T-shirts casual style.

"Right," said Jon, trying not to sound ungrateful.

"Button-downs are actually great," said Aunt Beverly, "especially if you add a colored T-shirt under them and wear khakis instead of these . . . hmmmm . . . 'church pants'?" We both laughed when she said "church pants." There's really no other name for them. Grandmother Turner had been sending Jon slacks that looked like the bottom half of a suit.

"But what can I do?" said Jon. "I don't want to hurt her feelings, and I know her sending me the clothes really helps out Dad. I know he's had lots of extra expenses since we moved here and

**9**

he bought into the Collinsville Family Fitness Center."

"Well, actually, Jon," said Aunt Beverly, "you have lots of good stuff in your closet. It's just a matter of filling in the missing pieces and learning how to put some looks together."

And then Aunt Beverly and I had the same idea flash into our minds at the same time. (That happens to us often.) We looked at each other and asked in unison, "Do you have any clothes from Grandmother Turner that you haven't worn yet?"

"Well," said Jon, surprised at this double-barreled onslaught of words from us, "I just got a packet last week and in it were these two shirts and two pairs of pants. I haven't even taken off the tags yet."

"Bring them along!" said Aunt Beverly. "We're about to introduce you to the wonderful world of exchanges!"

"Exchanges?" asked Jon.

"Turning in new clothes for *new* clothes," I explained. "You're going to like this a l-o-t."

And with that, we scooped up Grandmother Turner's packet and drove off to Benton with Jon.

Our first stop was Mr. Ray's. I was shocked at what a difference a half hour can make in the hands of a pro! Mr. Ray talked to Jon a little about his activities and what kinds of looks he liked, and then he started in with the scissors, a little mousse, a little blow-drying. Before my very eyes, Jon Weaver became one of the most handsome guys I've ever seen in my life—including the models in magazines.

Jon seemed in shock. He really didn't know what to say. I think he was excited and pleased and scared and embarrassed all at the same time. All he said was, "Am I going to be able to do this every morning?"

Mr. Ray assured him that with practice, he'd get close to the same look. "You were watching what I did, weren't you?" asked Mr. Ray.

"Of course!" said Jon with a grin. "Every move, like a hawk. That doesn't mean I can do what you did, though."

Mr. Ray gave Jon a couple of tips and a can of hairspray and then we left and went to Norton's. Aunt Beverly showed Jon the way around the exchange counter, and we headed up to the Young Men's department.

And with that, dear Journal, I'm going to have to say good night. It's late. But I promise I'll write tomorrow. There's a lot still to catch up on.

## Chapter Two

# Missing Pieces Found

*W*ell, here I am again, trying to catch up and finish all that I started to tell you last night.

Perhaps I should explain, first, the reason I'm so far behind. You see, dear Journal, I forgot you. Not forgot *about* you, but forgot you—as in left you behind in Eagle Point when we went there a couple of weeks ago for my graduation from junior high. You were a gift to me from my little sister, Kiersten. I know Aunt Beverly helped pick you out because with your wide navy and white stripes (with just a tiny narrow red stripe), you are a perfect match to my new swimsuit and cover-up outfit.

Anyway . . . Kiersten gave you to me as a gift at dinner before my graduation and since we needed to go directly to the graduation ceremony from the restaurant, I gave you to Aunt Beverly for safe-keeping. She put you in a drawer at the house and the next morning, neither of us remembered you . . . so you were left behind.

Fortunately for me, Aunt Beverly was planning to go back to Eagle Point last Sunday and Monday to visit an old friend there—a woman she hadn't seen in years, but whom she ran into while she was visiting a gallery in Eagle Point. Her friend, Madge Berry, was someone she had known at McKinney College when she and Mom were students there. They had a great time visiting but decided they still had lots more to talk about . . . so Aunt Beverly went over last Sunday after church and came home Monday about noon. Madge lives several states away now so it really was an unusual opportunity for them to visit.

I liked her a lot, what little I saw of her. She was tall and had auburn hair. That's the color that Kiersten is hoping her hair will turn someday. Right now, it's just plain red—in fact, in the summer sun, she's almost what you'd call a "strawberry blond." Madge had a wonderful smile and I loved the big floppy straw hat she was wearing. I found myself thinking, *Maybe this is someone that Dad should meet.* That thought really surprised me. It's the first time I've really thought of Dad meeting someone and dating her—and who knows, maybe even marrying her. Mom died almost a year and a half ago and I know Dad is lonely. It's hard to think of Dad with someone else, but I know that it would probably be the best thing for him someday.

After all, Aunt Beverly is the one who introduced Dad (her brother) to my mother (her best friend in college). So . . . who knows, perhaps she'll introduce Dad to someone else. Although I can't imagine anyone ever *really* taking the place of Mom.

It probably won't happen, though. Aunt Beverly said that Madge is only going to be in Eagle Point one more week. And that really isn't the point of my writing, anyway. I'm quite prone to rambling, I know. It's something I'm trying to work on.

The point is, Aunt Beverly brought you back from the house when she returned to Collinsville on Monday afternoon.

Since she was gone on Monday, I had the full responsibility for the store. Oh, Mrs. Campbell came in for a few hours to help—and to be totally honest with myself and you, Mrs. Campbell was probably *really* in charge, since I *am* just over fourteen and a half. Still, it felt as if I was in charge. I opened the store by myself and at the end of the day, balanced the cash register. I was only off two cents! (I took that out of my own purse so I'd have a perfect balance to show Aunt Beverly.)

I was too tired to write Monday night—running a shop all by yourself can really drain the energy right out of you. And then on Tuesday night, we had the first meeting of the FF Club. But now I'm getting ahead of myself.

Back to our shopping spree last week in Benton.

Aunt Beverly and Jon Weaver and I spent three entire hours in Norton's trying on clothes—all for him. He was a good sport about it. I hadn't really known if he'd go along with all the experimentation that I knew Aunt Beverly would want to do. In the end, we helped Jon pick out several new things in exchange for the clothes his Grandmother Turner had sent. He actually got more for his money, at least as far as I'm concerned—two pairs of walking shorts, a swimsuit, a pair of khaki slacks, and two plaid shirts (with collars, but not button-downs).

We had lunch at a place called Black-Eyed Willie's—a fun place for barbecue. We all had pulled pork sandwiches. They make their own french fries there, which was neat. They were delicious!

After lunch, we came back to Collinsville and went to the optometrist's office. Dr. Engler gave Jon a prescription for contact lenses, which Jon said that he has wanted for years. Aunt Beverly talked me into a new pair of frames for my reading glasses. They are very narrow gold wire-rims, but with great big lenses. Aunt Beverly commented, "They don't hide your beautiful eyes at all."

I don't know if she noticed, but it's Jon Weaver who has the beautiful eyes. He's got such long eyelashes. I'm a little jealous!

After the eye doctor, we went to Woodie's Shoe Store. They always have a great selection—as good as anything you can find in Benton—and I knew what Aunt Beverly was doing. Since she owns a shop in Collinsville, she likes to "shop the town," as she says it, so she can support her fellow merchants. It's too bad that Collinsville doesn't have a really great men's shop. Yearling's went out of business two years ago and nothing has come into town yet to take its place.

At Woodie's, Aunt Beverly helped Jon pick out a neat pair of sandals, some socks to go with a new pair of loafers, and also a new belt. The sacks were really beginning to pile up in the back of her car!

And then . . . we had one more stop. We went to McGreggor's, of all places.

"What are we doing here?" I asked.

"Well," said Aunt Beverly, "do you remember that big stack of white T-shirts that Jon had on the chest at the end of his closet?"

"They sell T-shirts at McGreggor's?" asked Jon.

"No," said Aunt Beverly, "but they sell dye." And with that, we went to the part of the store where the Rit dye boxes were stacked neatly—just like everything else in McGreggor's—and we went a little wild picking out colors!

"Your mission, should you choose to accept it," said Aunt Beverly, "is to give yourself some *color* this week."

"Will you help with the dying?" Jon asked me.

"Of course!" I said. "How about hot pink?"

We couldn't sell Jon on the idea of hot pink, but we did talk him into something called "salmon," and also boxes of "turquoise" and "sunshine yellow," which looked to me more like school-bus yellow, but I didn't say anything. I was afraid if I did, Jon would lose his color courage. We also got boxes of olive green, tan, and red. Jon's really going to be in for some color!

You can't go to McGreggor's without getting a soda, of course. At least, Aunt Beverly and I can't. So . . . the three of us plopped ourselves down on the stools along the well-worn counter and ordered the Weber special—chocolate sodas with chocolate ice cream. Jon isn't into chocolate like Aunt Beverly and I are, but he had to admit, that was the best soda he's ever had.

Mr. McGreggor waited on us, which is a bit unusual. Grandpa Stone told me one time that Sam McGreggor used to be the best soda jerk in the state. That was back when Sam first worked at McGreggor's, when it was his father's store. He and Grandpa are about the same age, and I think it's special that they both own stores in town and have been friends for more than sixty years.

We told Mr. McGreggor about what we were planning to do with the Rit dye and he looked at Jon and said, "These gals are really going to get you spruced up, aren't they?"

"More than you know," said Jon with a grin. "I'm their number-one guinea pig."

"And lovin' every minute of it, I can tell," said Mr. McGreggor, laying on a bit extra of his otherwise quite mild Scottish accent.

"You should be careful, lassies," he said with a wink to Aunt Beverly and me. "If you get him looking too handsome, other lassies might find him more attractive, too. You might not have counted on that."

We all laughed. But I must admit, dear Journal, I had *not* counted on that. Not at all. I've never seen Jon Weaver talk to any girl other than Libby and me—and Kimber and Trish, too—but we're all just friends. I'm not sure I like the idea of Jon Weaver having a girlfriend. Not that I *really* mind, of course. It would probably just mean that we couldn't spend quite so much time together.

Anyway . . .

On Wednesday and Thursday afternoons, Jon

came over to my house and Mrs. Miller helped us turn several of Jon's white T-shirts into a rainbow . . . well, sorta. The clothesline out back was certainly colorful.

While we worked, we talked a little about our ideas for the FF Club.

Jon admitted to me that he didn't like the name of the club the first time he heard it. "I'm into earning A's, not F's," said Jon. "I didn't like the idea of the F's being associated with failure."

"That isn't what it means at all!" I said.

"I know, I know," said Jon. "And I've come to see your point. I know you had in mind 'Forever Friends.' I think it's neat that the F's can refer to lots of other things, too—like 'future' and 'fantastic' and 'food' and 'fun' and 'faith' and 'forever' and 'food.' Did I already say 'food'?"

"You already said 'food.'"

"Well, you can never have too much of a good thing," said Jon with his typical grin. "And then, there's always the F for 'female'!"

"I'm surprised you didn't mention that twice," I teased. "So, what's your point? Do you think the club should have a different name? After all, there's FFA and FHA. Those organizations have F's in their names."

"So does the FCC and the FAA," said Jon. "No . . . I'm just letting you know that I'm fully supportive of the name—now. It's really a pretty cool name, the more you think about it."

"Speaking of all the F's . . . I've been thinking that the club just might have a theme for each month. Or if a month is too frequent, maybe each season of the year."

"Like what?" asked Jon.

"Like Feeling Fine—that could be a month when we all make a special effort to exercise and we could get together and have a time when we all shared our favorite health tips."

"Doesn't sound like a lot of fun," Jon said.

"It *could* be fun," I said, "if we *made* it fun. We could teach each other new jazzercize routines, maybe."

"How about if we took a bicycle trip . . . one that was twenty or thirty miles. We might even stay overnight."

"Now there's an idea!" I said. "But I'm not sure I could ride for twenty or thirty miles right now. That's almost to Benton!"

"That's the point," Jon said eagerly. "We could meet a few times—maybe two or three times a week for a couple of weeks—to ride different routes together, to build up our endurance."

"Yes!" I said. "I've got the vision! We could even have picnic dinners together—potluck style."

"But," said Jon, "I thought you said that the

purpose of the club was supposed to be service to others."

"I did," I said, "and I still think that's really important. I originally had in mind that we might go over to Crestwood Manor, the retired people's home, and teach the people there some simple exercises they could do to the old-timey music they like to listen to."

"That's a good idea," said Jon. I noticed that he said it with a little bit of hesitation in his voice.

"What's the matter?" I asked.

"Oh, nothing about the club," he said. "I was just looking at this T-shirt. I'm not sure about this color. I wasn't prepared for salmon to be quite so . . . orange."

"It is a bit bright. Maybe it'll seem less bright once the shirt dries," I said. "But back to the club . . . I really like your idea of the bicycle trip. What could we do, though, that would include community service?"

"W-e-l-l," said Jon. He must have strung out that "well" for ten seconds. "I've got it!" he said with a shout. "We could take garbage bags and pick up litter along the way."

"Great idea!" I said. "Grandpa Stone has some nailers down at the hardware store he'd probably loan us."

"Some what?" said Jon.

"That's what Kiersten and I call them. They're

sticks—poles, really—that have nail-like points at one end. They're for spearing litter."

"That's great. We might even find that we could ride along and get the litter without ever stopping to get off our bikes."

"Sounds like bicycle polo . . . well, sorta," I said.

"Yeah," said Jon. "This is getting better all the time."

About that time Trish came in. "Ooooh, hot peach," she said as she looked at the T-shirt we were rinsing out.

"Salmon," said Jon.

"It's a good thing you didn't say orange," I said.

Trish is big into T-shirts. She wears them all the time, along with her jeans shorts and baseball caps. That description makes Trish sound like a tomboy, but she really isn't. She just likes to dress very casually. Of all the friends I've made so far in Collinsville, Trish is probably the most athletic. Kimber is great at gymnastics—or at least that's the conclusion I've drawn from looking at all the trophies and ribbons in her room—but Trish is more into activities than Kimber. She's always game for a swim or a hike.

"How does a thirty-mile bicycle trip sound to you?" Jon asked.

"Sounds great," said Trish. "If one had a bicycle to ride thirty miles."

"You don't have a bike here, do you?" I said,

thinking out loud. "I'll bet you could borrow one from Stone's Hardware." Grandpa Stone just started carrying bicycles last year. He's been talking about giving me a new one. Maybe I could have him give it to me this summer so Trish could use it and I could ride my old one. Just a thought. I'll have to check on that possibility.

"That would be great," she said. "Where are we riding to?"

"We'll have to figure that out," I said.

"We need to have a meeting," added Jon. "Don't you think it's about time? If we're really going to have this club and do some of the things we've all talked about, we ought to get started."

"When?" I said.

After a little discussion, we decided that our first meeting would be next Tuesday, which was actually a few days ago. I really am behind in writing in you, dear Journal.

About that time, Mrs. Miller called to Trish that it was time for them to go home. "Be right there, Gram," said Trish. And then she whispered to me, "Do you suppose Tad Wilson likes to ride bikes?" Trish really is going to try to catch Tad's eye—I just know it. Even though he's a newly graduated senior, she just might have a shot at it. Jon even thought so. Trish would probably have my head if she knew that I had told Jon about Trish's crush on Tad Wilson. Jon agreed with me, though, that Trish has the kind of personality that makes her seem older. She's so sure of herself.

When Trish left the house with her grandmother, I noticed that she carried her grandma's bag and helped her into the car. Trish really seems to love her grandmother. It's probably the only reason she allowed herself to be brought to Collinsville in the first place. She certainly wasn't at all eager to leave her parents when we stopped to pick her up in Fruitvale a couple of weeks ago on our way back from Eagle Point.

In one way, it's strange to think of Mrs. Miller as Trish's grandmother. Mrs. Miller seems almost a part of *our* family! I know she's only been with us a few weeks, but it's been great. She fixes dinner for us each night and we haven't eaten this well, since . . . well, since Mom died. Mrs. Miller also cleans house for us and she likes to cut fresh flowers from the yard to put in the vase that's on the piano in the living room. Kiersten and I both nearly cried the first time we saw the flowers there. It really reminded us of Mom.

Back to my reporting on the current activities. That little talk with Trish was on Thursday. On Friday, I got in touch with Libby and Kimber. They were both excited about having the first meeting of the FF Club. And about the bike trip . . . at least Kimber was excited about the bike trip.

"Oh, K-k-k-katelyn," Libby had said. I think it

was the first time I had ever heard her stutter when she said my name, so I could tell she was upset. "I d-d-d-don't know if I can ride thirty m-m-m-iles."

"I don't know if I can either, Libby," I said. "That's why we're going to have several shorter rides for a few weeks—to build ourselves up to that point. It's not going to be a race. It's going to be a fun ride. And we'll be stopping a lot to pick up litter."

"L-l-l-litter?" she said.

"Right. That's the community service part of the ride."

"Sounds like l-l-l-loads of fun," she said with a groan.

"It will be!" I said. "You'll see."

Kimber was more into the idea, especially when I assured her that Dennis Anderson was going to be called about the first meeting of the FF Club, and that we'd all put high pressure on him to go on the bike trip. Every time I talk to Kimber, she asks me first thing, "Have you seen Dennis? Has Jon said anything about him?" She's really got it bad.

You can imagine how excited she was when Jon and Dennis showed up at youth group on Sunday.

But I'm getting a little ahead of myself. First, there's Friday night. That's when Jon and his father and Aunt Beverly and I all went to Tony's Pizza

Parlor for dinner. Aunt Beverly had stopped by to measure the windows at Jon's house just about the time Jon and I brought home all his newly dyed, clean and dried T-shirts. Aunt Beverly took a few minutes to show Jon how to put the T-shirts together with his button-down shirts for different looks.

Jon changed into one of the new shirts and a pair of khaki shorts for dinner. He looked great. Even his dad said, "I think I'm going to have to quit referring to you as little Jon." Both grinned.

On Saturday, I worked with Aunt Beverly in the shop and then Kiersten and I went over to Grandpa Stone's to watch a video with him and Dad. It was kind of an old movie called *The Bear*. It's really great, though—funny, and sad, and scary all at different times. Kiersten and I have seen it several times but we still like it. This was the first time for Grandpa Stone to see it. He liked it, too. We were glad about that. He hasn't seen many movies.

Then on Sunday morning, Kiersten and Dad and I went to church at Faith Community Fellowship. I've come to realize in the last few days that most of the people who go there call it simply F.C.F. I guess I'll call it that, too. It's pretty close to the FF Club, though. We sat with Kimber and Mari Chan and their parents. Mari had a new haircut. Kiersten has talked about nothing since. She would give anything if she had straight hair like Mari's instead of her full head of red curls. "I suppose you'd want it to be black hair," teased Dad.

"Yep," said Kiersten. "Could we dye my hair black—like Katelyn and Jon dyed his T-shirts different colors?"

"Don't even think about it," Dad said. "Besides, you're of Norwegian and German ancestry. Red hair is perfect for you. Mari is half-Chinese, half English. Black hair is right for her. To each his own."

"Her own," I said.

"Right," said Dad. "*Her* own." Dad gave me a big smile. He knows how I am about grammar and about nailing down details. "You'll make a good editor some day," he added.

"Novelist," I said.

And now . . . *that* brings me up to Sunday night. Jon and Dennis walked into youth group together. And since it was just about time to start, we sat down about the same time. Jon came to sit by me . . . and then to my surprise and Kimber's utter shock, Dennis walked in front of Jon and me and Kimber and sat down next to Kimber! She was so excited, but she handled it really well. I tried hard to hear all that Pastor Bert . . . well, technically, "Youth Pastor Bert" . . . was sharing in his devotional, but I could hardly keep from wondering what Kimber was thinking. And she, of course, could hardly concentrate because Dennis was sitting beside her. Jon was probably the only one who got the full message!

I did hear enough, though, to know that Bert was talking about King David, and how he had made lots of mistakes in his life, but that God loved him always and that David is called in the Bible "a man after God's own heart." That's a really neat phrase, isn't it? "A woman after God's own heart." That sounds like something wonderful to be on somebody's gravestone—or even better, a description in a newspaper about a famous novelist named Katelyn Weber! Pastor Bert said the thing that made David a man after God's own heart was that he always repented when he did something wrong. He always asked God to forgive him and to help him not to sin again. I've been thinking about that a lot since Sunday. If that's what it takes to be a woman after God's own heart, I think it's do-able.

Once again, dear Journal, I'm fading fast. And I still have so much to tell you! It will have to wait until tomorrow, though. Sleep is calling my name.

# Chapter Three

# Missing Pieces
# Nailed Down

**Saturday**
**10 A.M.**

*W*ow! This is really strange. I don't think I've ever written in a journal on a Saturday morning before.

On Saturdays, I usually work in The Wonderful Life Shop with Aunt Beverly. She said last night, however, that since I've worked there all week long, she wanted me to take Saturday off this week. Normally, I'll have Mondays off—which I guess means that I won't work next Monday. Last Monday, I worked while Aunt Beverly was at Eagle Point.

At least I can be assured of finally catching you up, dear Journal, on all the details of this past week.

Monday, like I said, was a busy day. I was just

**29**

too tired to write that night. And then Tuesday night was the first meeting of our FF Club!

It was really exciting. I felt like I was watching the birth of something.

There were seven of us gathered together in my living room downstairs. We finally decided that was the best place to have the first meeting, although we all agreed we need to come up with some kind of neutral meeting place. The seven "charter members"—that's what we agreed to call ourselves—are Kimber Chan, Libby Webster, Trish Martin, Dennis Anderson, Julio Martinez, Jon Weaver, and Katelyn Weber.

I was elected president and Jon was elected vice-president. Libby was elected secretary-treasurer. We officially named the club the "Forever Friends Club"—FF for short. And we told Libby to put a special note in the minutes stating that the name of the club had originally been her idea.

We made several important decisions.

First, we decided that any high school student who lives in Collinsville—whether they go to Collinsville High or East Valley High—can be in the club.

Then we decided that membership dues should be five dollars every two months. That will give us money for fun activities and also for community service projects. We all pitched in our five dollars, so we now have thirty-five dollars in our club account. We agreed that the best place we knew to keep the money right now—especially since it's not all that much—is in the safe at Aunt Beverly's shop. Maybe someday we'll open a bank account.

We agreed that anybody can join or drop out of the club at any time. We talked about having club T-shirts with our club name on them, and we decided that we would like to figure out a way to require that former members not wear the T-shirts. We couldn't reach a decision, so we decided to talk about it at the next meeting.

And then we made a formal motion—it passed seven to nothing—that the purpose of the club would be to provide community service to Collinsville. We all admitted, of course, that we intend to have lots of fun together as friends while we give to the town, but we wanted it clear from the beginning that FF isn't primarily a social club.

We talked for a while about how we might get other kids to be a part of the club. Kimber, for example, asked if she should have called Marcia and Sam about our first meeting. We felt a little bad that we hadn't called them, especially since they had been at the slumber party when we first talked about the idea. We all agreed that they could still be called charter members if they join.

Jon and Dennis both said that they knew of

two or three other guys who might be interested in joining. (That was good news to us girls!)

Finally, we talked about the bike trip. That was the first that Dennis or Julio had heard about the trip, but they were really excited about it. They started talking right away about how many practice rides we should have, how long they should be, what we needed to do to make sure all of our bicycles were in good working order, and so on. We agreed to meet next Tuesday night to go over routes that we might start riding together. We each have an assignment before our next meeting.

Jon and Dennis are going to find maps and come up with a few suggestions on routes. Julio is going to bring his bike-repair kit. He's apparently quite a mechanic. That's good to know!

I'm going to work on a schedule of practice rides and ask Grandpa Stone about the nailers to pick up litter. Kimber is going to see where we can get the best buy on trash bags. Libby is going to figure out the plans for the picnic dinners. And Trish is going to make some calls to see where we might get some T-shirts made with the name of our club on them. Kimber is also going to work on a design for the T-shirts.

Once we were finished with our business meeting, we dove into the chocolate cake that Mrs. Miller had made just for our first meeting. "Don't count on a cake each week," she had said, "but a new club should have a great dessert for its first meeting, don't you think?" What I think is that her chocolate cake was the best I've ever tasted! Not only was it three layers high and lathered in rich chocolate frosting, but she had put "FF" on the top with red icing.

"I hereby suggest that we adopt red and brown as our official club colors," said Trish as we finished up the last crumbs of the cake. It didn't take long for seven of us to finish the entire thing—along with a gallon of milk!

We all laughed at Trish's suggestion. But the more we talked about it as a serious idea, the more it seemed like a good one—at least nobody had any better ideas. "And chocolate as our official club flavor!" she added. Again, we had no protests. Mrs. Miller seemed really pleased when I told her.

And there you have it—the birth of a club.

One of the best parts of the evening, though, had nothing really to do with the club. It had to do with Jon.

Jon got his contact lenses on Tuesday morning, so Tuesday night was the first chance he had to really pull his entire new look together. You should have seen everybody's face when he walked into the room. He had on his newly-dyed turquoise T-shirt, khaki shorts, and sandals. His hair had turned out as well as when Mr. Ray did it, and without glasses—the jaws all dropped!

"Hey, stud man," said Dennis.

"I think we can no more be calling you Mr. Four-Eyes," said Julio in his best . . . well, craziest anyway . . . Indian accent. Julio has this thing about pretending to be from India. He told us at the Wilsons' swim party that one time a woman had asked him what part of India he was from—I guess in a way, with his dark skin and dark hair, he does look a little as if he could be from India. Anyway, Julio had faked an Indian accent and made up an extravagant tale about his home on the border between India and Pakistan, and about the persecution from the Pakistanis that had brought him and his family to America. When the woman had volunteered, however, to call upon his mother to offer the family assistance, Julio had been forced to confess his lie. "Hardest confession I ever made," he said.

Julio is anything but Indian. He actually is "a true Mexican," according to him . . . but even that isn't entirely true. Julio's father is of Spanish descent and his mother is of Indian heritage—the North American variety. They met while they were both students at the medical school at Guadalajara, Mexico. They fell in love and married during their third year. Julio was born there two months after his mother graduated from medical school, which is where he gets the "Mexican" bit. He's actually an American citizen since both of his parents are Americans. Both of them are also doctors now. Julio's father is a specialist in ear, nose, and throat—an otorhinolaryngologist. He works in Benton. Julio's mother is in family practice with two other women here in Collinsville. Anyway . . . for fun, Julio still likes to put on his Indian accent. He's really quite good at it. And we all know it's just for fun.

Kimber, Trish, and Libby were stunned at Jon's appearance and have been talking about it for days. "I think I need to t-t-t-talk to your Aunt Beverly about a m-m-m-make-over," said Libby.

"You don't need one," said Trish. "You always look great." I think Libby was really surprised and pleased at Trish's comment. Trish never says anything she doesn't mean. And Libby can use a little boost to her confidence.

Jon, of course, tried to act super cool and nonchalant—that's a new word I just learned. (Isn't it great? I just had to use it.) He just shrugged off all the compliments from everybody, but I could tell he was really pleased.

He was the last to leave and as he got ready to walk out the door I said, "The Weave has arrived." He just smiled.

"I d-o-o-o-o like that name," he said, grinning. "But I don't think I look all *that* different."

"No?" I said, teasing him. "Get a mirror, Jon

Weaver. You were always good-looking, but now you're male-model material."

"That's what I thought about you when you changed your looks and showed up at the Wilsons' party looking so beautiful," he said. His voice was very tender and serious. I could tell I was on the verge of blushing so I quickly said, "And now? All the magic's gone, right? And so soon."

"Hardly," said Jon. He still sounded serious and I'm not sure I can handle a serious Jon Weaver. I do better talking to the guy with the grin.

"See you," I said, closing the front door behind him.

On Wednesday just before noon, I called Jon at Stone's Hardware—he's working there in the mornings now, helping Dad develop a complete inventory system for the store—and then I met him there during lunch so we could bring the sixth chair of their new dining set back up to Aunt Beverly's shop. I was relieved to find Jon had returned to his teasing, grinning self. After work, Mr. Clark Weaver and Jon loaded the table and chairs into the back of their van and Aunt Beverly and I followed them home so Aunt Beverly could tell the guys *precisely* where to put the table.

"Now you have a place to put those new candle holders and candles you bought several weeks ago," Aunt Beverly said.

"Right," said Mr. Clark Weaver. "Which reminds me about dinner. How does seven o'clock on Saturday night sound to you? I know a little place in Benton I'd like to take you. Not too fancy, but a few notches up from Burger Haven."

"Sounds great," said Aunt Beverly.

Jon looked at me and with woeful eyes and a tone of fake dismay, he said, "And what shall we orphans do?"

"You can come over to our house for dinner," I said. "Mrs. Miller always makes more than enough, and besides, Aunt Beverly won't be there."

"That's right," chimed in Aunt Beverly. "You can eat my portion of the nightly fare."

"Oh, I had in mind a real splurge," said Jon Weaver. "How about Mexico Pete's?"

Aunt Beverly caught my eye and it was all I could do to keep from laughing. She may not be going to Manor House, but *I* am going to Mexico Pete's! The difference, of course, is that Aunt Beverly's Saturday night is a date. Mine is only dinner with a good friend.

Thursday and Friday were just sort of average days at the shop, I guess. Business was really brisk on Thursday. (I just love that word "brisk." It's a word Gramma Weber uses a lot.) We had a tour bus stop by—a group of people en route to Eagle Point and Castle Rock. Aunt Beverly thinks that's the first tour bus she's ever seen stop at The Wonderful Life Shop. It was really crowded for a while, but the people were all very friendly and they didn't seem to mind. In fact, I think they rather liked the fact that it was so crowded. One thing's for sure—they cleaned out Aunt Beverly's supply of little silver frames, her potpourri pillows, and nearly all of her new embroidered pillowcases. She spent a good portion of Friday morning on the phone reordering from some of the suppliers she met on her last buying trip.

I realized in talking to Aunt Beverly on Friday that I haven't been spending much time with Kiersten, so we're going to the pool together this afternoon. No Mari. No Kimber. Just Kiersten and me. It's been a while since we did anything alone together. I'm really looking forward to it. You never can tell what Kiersti is going to say next—or what she might ask!

# Chapter Four

# Splish, Splash!

The Collinsville Club is, without a doubt, one of my favorite places on all the earth . . . even though I realize I haven't seen all the earth . . . yet! It's a club Grandpa Stone has belonged to for years and years. In fact, I think his father, my great-grandfather, helped to found it.

Originally, the Collinsville Club was called the Collinsville *Country* Club. Grandpa said that was really true in the old-timey days—the club was in the *country*. He said that the city people wanted a place where they could get away from their own neighborhoods and the bustle of downtown, ride out into the country, and enjoy a little game of croquet with their friends. A nine-hole golf course was added later when the Milwee farm was pur-

**39**

chased by the club. And then a swimming pool and tennis courts were added. The croquet lawn is still there, as well as a grass-bowling lawn. Grandpa said people have started to play both games more in recent years. There's also a horse-shoe pitch. Out beyond the golf course is an area that's set up for horse riding—English style—and the stables, of course.

All of which sounds very snooty, but that isn't the atmosphere of the Collinsville Club. The club is now in the north part of town, which is just a few blocks—a mile maybe—north of the downtown district, which is where we live, and where Grandpa Stone and Aunt Beverly live, too. Most of the members are average people just like us. Actually, Collinsville doesn't have very many rich people—at least, not that you can tell by their houses or cars or anything.

Anyway . . . the "club," as we call it, is one of my favorite places. It has lots and lots of big old trees, which means there's lots of shade, except in the area of the tennis courts and pool. Even there, big trees are part of the gardens just next to the pool, so the pool has partial shade late in the after-noon. I think the thing that I like the most is the feeling that everybody is very relaxed and friendly. Nobody is out to prove anything to anybody else or to try to convince people they have an edge in life. People come to the club for a little sun, a little fun, and a little relaxation. That makes for a pretty nice atmosphere.

Plus, the club has the best cherry limeades in the whole world . . . at least in Collinsville, McGreggor's included. They still serve them at the Poolside Snack Bar with a little tiny paper umbrella and a maraschino cherry. Kiersten and I always get one when we come. Neither one of us has ever grown tired of cherry limeades—and I doubt if we ever will!

Plus, the club has the biggest, fluffiest towels I've ever seen. They are white and soft and have a smell all their own—some sort of flower, I think. Sitting by the pool on a Collinsville Club beach towel, leaning back against a padded beach half-chair, sipping a cherry limeade, and soaking up the sun, is about the best feeling I can imagine.

And that's precisely what I was doing at about two o'clock Saturday afternoon when a cup of cold water was poured on my head. I couldn't believe it! There's nothing more shocking to the system, believe me, than to be sitting enjoying the warmth and pleasure of life and then rudely jolted by ice tumbling over one's shoulders! I knew it wasn't Kiersten because I had been watching her in the pool. But who? I whirled around to see . . . Julio!

"Julio!" I sputtered. "That's downright cruel!"

"Sorry," he said as he plopped down beside me.

"I just couldn't resist." He helped me pick up stray ice cubes and toss them into the pool.

"Well, I may forgive you," I said, "but you'll have to check with me next year."

"That long, huh? If I'd known, I would only have poured out half the cup," he replied. "Begging your pardon, missy," he added, in his best fake Indian accent.

Turning more serious, he said, "I didn't know that you were a member here."

"Grandpa Stone is, and I think he worked out something so that we can be considered his 'family.' He and Dad are out on the golf course."

"You don't play golf, huh?" he asked.

"Not really. I can putt pretty well. Frankly, I didn't know that Grandpa and Dad played until I asked them just last week. They said they both knew how to play and that they love the game, but that they hadn't played in a long, long time. The next thing I knew, Grandpa was digging two sets of golf clubs out of his garage, and he and Dad were cleaning them up at the kitchen table. Who knows how high their scores are going to be!"

"Are you here at the pool alone, then?" he asked.

"No," I said and before I could explain, Julio asked, "Is Jon here, too?"

"Jon?" I asked. "Why would you think, of all my friends, that Jon would be here?"

"Well, you two seem like an item," he said.

"Wrong conclusion," I said. "Jon and I are just great friends. We both started in at Collinsville High late in the year and we were seated next to each other. The rest of the kids kinda ignored us at first, so we got to be friends. Actually, I'm here with my little sister, Kiersten."

"I didn't know you had a sister," said Julio. "I'm here with my little sister, too—and brother. Vincent is over there at the diving board . . . the next one in line . . . and Carmen is paddling around in the baby pool. She's only three."

"She's darling," I said. Carmen really is a cutie. She has short chubby legs and big round cheeks and even though she was all alone in the shallow wading pool that's next to the main pool, she was having the time of her life splashing around and jumping under—and then out from under—the fountain that's at the center of the pool. "She really knows how to have a good time," I added. "Little sisters are good at that, I think."

"Which one is your sister?" Julio asked.

I pointed Kiersten out to him. "See the skinny little redhead in the green-and-white polka-dotted suit? The one playing dive-for-the-penny with those two boys? That's my Kiersti."

"Those boys are my cousins, Mario and Richard! They're visiting us from California for a week. I thought they were playing with Vincent, but it looks like they found somebody more fun!" Julio teased.

"Kiersten is that," I said.

"You really love her a lot, don't you?" Julio said.

"I really do," I replied. "Kiersten is probably the best little sister a girl could ever have—that is, when she's not asking a million questions." Really, when I stop to think about it, Kiersten is getting a lot better about asking questions. At least she seems to be waiting for an answer occasionally before diving into the next question. "In the first place, she adores me and would never pour a cup of ice water on my head," I added, teasing a bit. "In the second place, she's just plain fun. I don't think Kiersten ever met a stranger or has been at a loss for words in her entire life. She was born talking."

"Carmen, too," said Julio. "She doesn't have a big vocabulary yet, of course, but she sure knows how to use the words she *does* know."

"Kiersten is the one who introduced me to Kimber Chan. Kiersti and Kimber's little sister, Mari, are friends. On the first day that we moved to Collinsville, Kiersti rode her bike all over the neighborhood, as she tells it, 'until I found a friend.'"

"Pretty bold move for a little girl new to town," said Julio.

"I didn't make a friend for three weeks!" I said.

"That's one of the differences between Kiersti and me."

"Is Kimber the reason that you and your family go to Faith Community Fellowship?" Julio asked.

"Right. We probably would have gone to the Baptist church otherwise. That's where Grandpa Stone attends—and has for years and years."

"That's where my parents go!" said Julio.

"I wondered about that," I said. "That is, if your parents went to church."

"Oh, yes," he said. "But they weren't always Baptists. When I was little, we all went to a different church. Then Dad and Mom went to a Billy Graham crusade when I was about seven or eight. I went, too. I still remember the huge crowd of people and the fact that hardly anybody moved around when Billy Graham spoke. That really impressed me."

"It's funny, isn't it, how things like that stick in your mind when you're a kid," I said.

"Yeah," said Julio. "I had been to that same stadium for a football game just a week before the crusade and I was really frustrated at all the people who kept moving around, blocking my view. I was pretty impressed that this time at the stadium, nobody moved."

"At least until the end of the service," I said.

"Right," said Julio. "Have you ever been to a Billy Graham meeting?"

"No," I said, "but I've watched the crusades on TV with my Grandpa. He makes it a point to watch Dr. Graham."

"Well, back to the reason why we're Baptists—at the end of Billy Graham's sermon, lots of people went forward to receive Christ into their lives—and my parents went, too. I tagged along, of course. And from that time on, we went to the Baptist church."

"Makes sense," I said.

"If your grandpa goes to the Baptist church, why don't you go there?" Julio asked.

"Well, Dad didn't think he wanted to go there, at least not right now. That's where he and my mother were married and he thought the memories might still be pretty painful for him."

"Are your parents divorced?" Julio asked. I could tell he was concerned as soon as he asked that maybe he had overstepped his bounds.

"No," I said. "My mother died in an automobile accident about a year and a half ago."

"I'm really sorry," said Julio. "That's hard."

"Yes, it has been," I said, "but I don't mind talking about my mother. She was a wonderful woman and I hope I grow up to be like her."

"If she was like you, she was a great lady," said Julio. I think that's the first time, dear Journal, that I have ever associated Julio Martinez with

Latin charm. He was oozing with it at that moment.

"There's a contradiction here somewhere," I teased. "Great ladies don't have ice water dumped on them."

"I said I was sorry," Julio moaned. "Are you going to hold that over my head the rest of my life?"

"I'd like to hold a cup of cold water over your head right now!" I quipped. *Trish would have been proud of that one-liner,* I thought.

"How about if I buy you a cherry limeade to make it up to you?" he asked.

"Sounds great," I said, "but I've already had one. I probably shouldn't have a second."

"You'll have time to recover your appetite by dinner," he said. And that, dear Journal, is how I came to bring home *two* little Chinese paper drink umbrellas.

Julio brought back the drinks from the Poolside Snack Bar, and as he handed me mine, he asked, "Are you going to youth group tomorrow night?"

"I'm planning to," I said. "Are you?"

"I'm going to try to make it. Jon called me yesterday about it. Dennis is going."

"Great."

"Maybe we could all go out together afterwards," said Julio. "As I understand it, Dennis has permission to drive his dad's car there."

"I didn't know he had his license!" I said.

"He just got it last week on his birthday."

"You mean, Dennis Anderson turned sixteen and nobody did or said anything about it? We could have really celebrated at the FF Club meeting!" I said.

"We didn't know until yesterday," said Julio. "Maybe we can throw him a belated-birthday party."

"There's an idea," I said, and the wheels started turning inside my mind. "We could call it a surprise party—as in surprise, it's l-a-t-e!"

"Good idea!" Julio said.

We talked for a few minutes about what we might do for a party and decided that the best time for it would be after youth group—which is tonight. As you can imagine, I've been scrambling in the last twenty-four hours to try to pull it all together. In fact, I've got to take a break here and get the cake out of the oven!

*still Sunday*
*4 P.M.*

Well, the cake is done, cooled, and frosted. With time out for a couple of phone calls, too. I'm determined to try to finish telling you all, dear Journal.

As we were planning Dennis's party, Julio just casually mentioned the first of two major facts of the afternoon. He said, "Dennis really likes Kimber, you know."

"Kimber really likes Dennis," I said.

"Do you think Kimber knows that Dennis likes her?" said Julio.

"Do you think Dennis knows that Kimber really likes him?" I said.

"Maybe we should do a little matchmaking at this party," said Julio.

"Don't do anything that would embarrass Kimber," I said. "P-l-e-a-s-e."

"I'll try not to," said Julio. "I can't have both of you on my case."

We both laughed at that. Then Julio said, "Let's see . . . Kimber and Dennis like each other. You and Jon are just friends. I don't have a girlfriend. What about Libby?"

"She doesn't have a crush on anybody right now," I said. "At least as far as I know."

"And Trish?"

"Well," I said, "Trish has a crush on somebody, but he's not in the FF Club."

"Good—I mean, if she did, it could get complicated!" Julio said.

"As in, it would have to be you?" I teased.

"I wouldn't mind," said Julio. "Trish is a great gal. I'm just trying to figure out the social dynamics here, as they say. It's looking as if Libby and I are going to have to be 'just friends' so we can hang out stag together."

"'Hang out stag together'?" I asked.

"That's a phrase my father used to use," said Julio. "I think it means being alone, but being alone with somebody. I'm not sure." Then Julio switched gears and asked, "Who is it that Trish likes?"

"I'm not sure I should say," I said, and then decided Trish probably wouldn't mind since Julio was a part of the FF Club and all. "Do you remember Tad Wilson, the son of the people who hosted the swim party a couple of weeks ago?"

"*That* Tad Wilson?" said Julio, dropping the second piece of bombshell news of the afternoon, as he pointed toward Tad Wilson sitting across the pool from us.

"What's he doing here?" I asked. "He *has* a great pool in his backyard."

"He comes here because of Cindy, I think," said Julio.

"Cindy?" I asked.

"Yes, the girl who is working in the Poolside Snack Bar."

At just that moment, Cindy—the beautiful, tall, slender, dark-haired Cindy—walked from behind the snack bar, took off the big shirt she had been wearing behind the snack bar and tossed it into Tad's lap, and raced toward the pool and dove in. Tad quickly got up and dove in after her, grabbing her by the arms as she came up from her dive. It was plain to see that they were a couple.

And so, dear Journal—there's a problem for us to sort out. Do I tell Trish or not?

One thing I *do* realize is that I'm not going to be able to tell you what happened next until tomorrow night. Otherwise, I won't be ready for youth group on time.

Who would have thought three months ago that my first summer in Collinsville would be so busy!

# Chapter Five

# A Night on the Town

*I*'m determined . . . absolutely, positively, unequivocally (isn't that a *great* word!) determined . . . that I am going to finally catch up with tonight's writing—even if I have to stay up until midnight and write by flashlight under the covers!

Back to the pool on Saturday afternoon . . . Cindy's dive into the pool gave Kiersten and her newly made friends, Mario and Richard, the idea that Julio and I also needed to be in the pool, rather than sitting on the sidelines. When we resisted their invitation to come in and play, we were splashed into submission. For the next hour or so, we played a pool version of Simon Says—doing cannonball jumps from the diving board, swimming with different strokes, and so forth. Vincent came and joined us, as well as a girl named Carla and another boy named Peter. It turned out to be lots of laughs.

We sorta "took over" the pool with our game. We didn't really mean to do that, but it just happened. One group of kids went home with their parents, who apparently had been playing tennis. An older man who was swimming laps finished his exercise. (When he got out, I realized it was Mr. Jacobson, the owner of the only real book and music shop in town. Some people think that Aunt Beverly's shop is a bookstore, but it's a lot more than that.) Tad and Cindy also got out of the pool and it was more obvious than ever that Tad is thoroughly smitten with Cindy. She seemed a little bit more distant toward him, but perhaps she was just flirting. I'm not an expert on these things. And . . . after all . . . I was trying to spy out the situation while playing Simon Sez!

Dad and Grandpa showed up at about 4:30 and it was a good thing they came when they did. I had totally lost track of the time. I was supposed to be ready to go with Jon to Mexico Pete's at six o'clock!

I was scrambling when I got home, as you can imagine. Hair to rinse and dry, then to curl. Makeup to put on. An outfit to iron. And a last-minute panic when I couldn't find one of my sandals. Kiersten finally cornered Scooter, who was happily gnawing away on it on the back porch. I was in too much of a hurry to scold him very severely. Actually, he hadn't done too much damage.

Fortunately, everything turned out OK by the time Jon rang the front doorbell at *exactly* six o'clock. Sometimes I just get lucky that way with my hair.

"Are all computer experts always so punctual?" I asked as I opened the screen door for Jon to come in.

"No," said Jon. "Just hungry ones."

"Mexico Pete's, is it?" said Dad as he rounded the corner and greeted Jon.

"I've never had my fill of greasy tacos," said Jon.

"Guess Kiersti and I will have to hit Tony's one more time this week," said Dad, grabbing Kiersten and giving her a big hug. That would suit Kiersten just fine. She's never had *her* fill of pepperoni pizza!

One of the best things about living in the downtown district is that all the downtown shops are within walking distance. I only have to walk about four blocks in any one direction and I can be just about anywhere I want to be. Two blocks one way and we're at the high school. Three blocks over and we're at the edge of downtown, which has only one major street (Main, of course), and two smaller side streets that come into Main at angles—Elm and Pine. The rest of the downtown streets are numbered. I'll draw you a little map.

You can see that Mexico Pete's is at 6th and Pine. Which means, of course, that it's just about as "downtown" as you can get.

There's a second shopping area out in the River Gorge area of town, and another much bigger shopping area out in East Valley. The downtown stores and restaurants, however, are my favorites.

It took Jon and me about twenty minutes to get to Mexico Pete's. We stopped for a few seconds in front of Aunt Beverly's shop so I could show Jon the new little porcelain animals that Aunt Beverly let me arrange into a display in the front window.

We also stopped for a minute so I could see what Clara's had in its display windows. Jon, teasing me, insisted that we *also* stop for a few moments in front of Stone's Hardware so he could gaze at the wheelbarrows and riding lawn mower. Crazy guy.

One of the best things about being with Jon is that we can talk about nearly anything and everything. He's just as easy to talk to as Kimber or Trish or Libby. While we had dinner—I ordered the number 4 platter with two tacos and rice, and Jon had the Mucho Grande platter with a taco, enchilada, tamale, relleno, and rice and beans—I told him about seeing Julio at the Collinsville

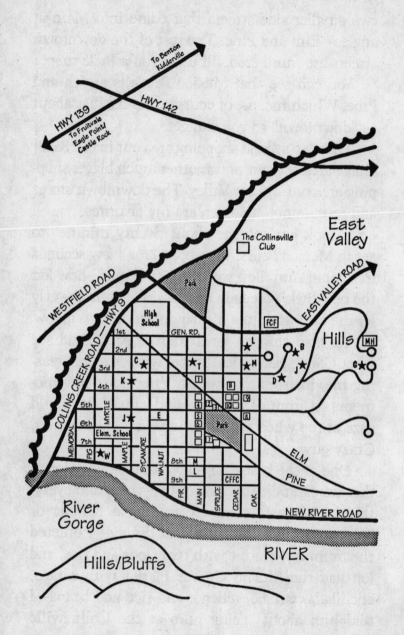

# Collinsville

| | |
|---|---|
| K = Katelyn | 1. The Wonderful Life Shop |
| J = Jon | 2. Clara's |
| B = Aunt Beverly | 3. Stone's Hardware |
| G = Grandpa | 4. McGreggor's |
| C = Kimber/Mari | 5. Jacob's Grocery |
| T = Trish | 6. McMillan's Jewelry |
| L = Libby | 7. Mexico Pete's |
| W = Wilsons | 8. Tony's Pizza |
| D = Dennis | 9. Burger Haven |
| M = Milners | 10. Woodie's |
| J = Julio | |

B = Baptist Church
E = Episcopal Church
M = Methodist Church
L = Lutheran Church
MH = Manor House
CFFC = Collinsville Family Fitness Center
FCF = Faith Community Fellowship

Club and about the party we had planned for Dennis. I also told him about seeing Tad Wilson with a girl named Cindy. Jon said that he thinks it's better if I tell Trish everything I know. He put it this way, "The longer you wait and the more she gets her hopes up, the more she's going to be hurt." He's probably right, but I'd rather not say anything and hope that Trish gets over her crush.

Jon also told me about a couple of other kids that he thinks might like to join the FF Club. He said they are kids he met while working at Stone's, which really surprised me.

"I thought you were supposed to be holed up in the office at Stone's, your head buried in the computer, entering inventory codes," I said.

"Most of the time, that's a pretty good description of what I'm doing!" said Jon. "But in order to double-check the codes, I sometimes need to get out on the floor. I was out checking on a code when this guy and gal asked me if I could ring up the sale of a birdbath."

"A birdbath?" I said. "I didn't know Grandpa had birdbaths. In a hardware store?"

"They're new. Over in the yard and garden tools area. He also ordered in some bird feeders, birdseed, and a couple of birdhouse kits. He said your Aunt Beverly had suggested he diversify a bit."

"Well, Aunt Beverly has great business sense.

At least that's what Grandpa Stone and Dad are always saying," I added.

"One birdbath sure sold in a hurry, at least," said Jon. "I couldn't find a clerk who wasn't busy so I rang up the sale for them. My first sale!"

"I didn't know you knew anything about the cash register," I said.

"Your dad showed me how to work it the first day," said Jon. "It's tied into the computer system so that all of the entries are cross-referenced."

"That makes sense," I said. "I hadn't thought about the computer part. Maybe Aunt Beverly needs to have a system like that. What do you think?"

"It might save her some time," said Jon. "Perhaps I should talk to her about it."

"I'll mention it, too," I said. "But back to the kids you met."

"Oh, yeah," said Jon, adding with a grin, "you sure have an amazing way of getting me side-tracked."

"I know," I said. "I ramble a bit. It's not a particularly good trait for a writer to have. It's something I'm trying to work on."

"Their names are Linda and Ford Milner," said Jon.

"Ford?" I asked. "Like the car?"

"He said it was short for Wilford," said Jon. And

we both laughed as we said simultaneously, "I'd go by Ford, too."

"They are brother and sister. They had come into Stone's to get a birthday present for their mother, who, according to them, has always wanted a birdbath. Linda's going to be a junior and Ford a sophomore. They go to East Valley, but they live pretty close to downtown. They seemed interested in the FF Club."

"That's a lot of information for just selling them a birdbath," I said.

"Oh," said Jon, with a grin, "didn't I say we had lunch? It was right at noon when they came in, which is why I couldn't find a free sales clerk. Two of the clerks had gone to lunch. One of them came back just as I was finishing the sale, and he commented that McGreggor's had a great deal on a burger and soda combo. Ford said that sounded great to him and asked me where McGreggor's was. I told them I'd show them, since I was thinking about going there for lunch, too. So we all went together."

"Did you invite them to the next FF Club meeting?" I asked.

"I told them I'd get in touch with them. I wasn't sure this next meeting was a good one for them to attend. It might be best if they started coming when we begin the bike rides."

"Whatever you think, Mr. Vice-President," I said.

"I thought you'd see it that way, Madam President," he said, still grinning that great Jon Weaver grin.

By this time, of course, we had finished dinner but Jon said that the Mucho Grande had made him too mucho full to move. So we sat and finished our iced tea and talked until it was nearly eight o'clock.

"Dad's going to wonder how long it takes to eat tacos," I said when I noticed the time.

"Do you think you should call him?" Jon asked. I thought that sounded like a good idea so I gave a quick call home. Dad and Kiersten had just returned from Tony's and everything was fine with Dad. He did suggest that we get back before dark.

On the way home, we had an unbelievably bad scene. I keep trying to erase it from my mind but it just won't go away.

It wasn't anything between Jon and me, thank goodness. But . . . between us and the guys that I'm now going to call "The Four Creeps." Jon told me their real names later in the evening: Dirk, Jim, Paul, and Skip.

It all started out innocently enough. Jon and I were walking out as they were walking in. Jon opened the door for me to walk out of Mexico Pete's and there they stood. When they saw it was

Jon and me, they just bunched up and blocked the door.

"Going somewhere, weevil?" sneered Dirk.

"Hey . . . the weevil got a new haircut," added Jim, with an equal amount of hatred in his voice. "Trying to look cool, huh?"

"Come on in," said Jon, motioning for them to go in while he held the door open for them.

"No more glasses, either," said Paul, totally ignoring what Jon had said. "He must be making a real s-e-r-i-o-u-s attempt at trying to be normal."

"Won't work," said Skip, who really got in Jon's face with that remark, so much so that Jon had to back up a step. "Once a nerd, always a nerd." Then he put one finger under the ribbing at the top of Jon's T-shirt and pulled it out, as if to snap it back into place.

"That's right," added Dirk. "Clothes can't change nerdiness."

"What's your problem, anyway?" asked Jon.

"You, weevil," said Paul, almost as if he was spitting out the words.

"And what have I done to you?" asked Jon, looking them right in the eye. I could tell he was really trying hard not to antagonize them, but I also noticed that his fists were clenched and a vein was starting to stand out on his neck.

"You're using up oxygen I'd like to breathe," said Dirk again, obviously assuming the ringleader role. He started faking a gag and Jim, Paul, and Skip quickly joined him.

Jon grabbed my hand and started to move forward, as if to walk through them out onto the street. When he did, Dirk pushed him back into Mexico Pete's so that he crashed into the first table and sent two of the chairs tumbling over.

"The trash goes out the back door," said Jim, who came in and stood over Jon.

I know that Jon could have taken any one of them on in a fight and done very well, thank you very much. None of The Four Creeps is all that big or strong looking. But four at once? Nobody could handle that.

I looked around quickly to see where Mexico Pete might be but all I saw were two wide-eyed waitresses.

"Come on, Jon," I said. "The back door suits me just fine." With one eye toward The Four Creeps, I also added—much to my horror now, "The back door is also the fire escape and it's so hot in here all of a sudden, I know something straight from hell just walked through the front door."

My comments stunned The Four Creeps just long enough for Jon to scramble to his feet, dust himself off, and add, speaking directly to Dirk, "I see your point."

And with that, he took my hand and we walked boldly and decisively—something I'm very good at—all the way to the back screen door and out into the alleyway.

Behind us, I heard Mexico Pete say, "What are you punks doing? Leave. Right now." *Where were you sixty seconds earlier?* I thought.

I know Mexico Pete has the size to back up his words. Peter Svensen isn't the swarthy, barrel-chested Mexican honcho you might be imagining, dear Journal. What he is, is a very tall, brawny Scandinavian guy who happens to love Mexican food. He's six feet six in his stocking feet—or so I heard Grandpa Stone say one day—with shoulders about five feet wide . . . or so they seem. I immediately knew that The Four Creeps had met their match.

Still, Jon and I didn't waste any time in making our exit. Neither one of us was interested in hanging around any longer. We didn't run, but we weren't walking slowly either, as we made our way down the short alleyway onto the street, and then over to Main. Neither one of us said a word until we got to Main Street. It was then that Jon let go of my hand. (In a way, it seemed more natural for him to be holding it. I guess I was more scared than I had let on—certainly far more scared than my words had conveyed to Dirk, Jim, Paul, and Skip.)

"That isn't the end of it," said Jon.

"There's really no point in retaliating," I said.

"One of my Gramma Weber's favorite Bible verses is Hebrews 10:30, the one that says, 'Vengeance is Mine, I will repay.'"

"I'm not thinking of retaliating," said Jon. "I'm not planning on doing *anything* with regard to those guys. They aren't worth the time or energy. What I'm more concerned about is getting you home safely. Those guys were just kicked out of Mexico Pete's."

"And?" I said.

"And . . . ," Jon continued, "I think those guys are going to be even more angry at us, and they may come looking for us. After all, they found us once before on the street where we both live."

I must admit, at that point I got a little scared. I turned around and as I did, I heard a car squeal around the corner just beyond Mexico Pete's.

"Let's go," I said, taking Jon's hand again and starting to run. We dodged into the side alleyway between Jacob's Grocery and McMillan's Jewelry Shop, and over to the next street. When I heard the car squeal around yet another corner just as we got to the Episcopal church, I said to Jon, "In here." I darted into the little courtyard and over into the cemetery area next to the church, and there we huddled behind the stone wall for a second to catch our breath. We had just about recovered from our mad dash—made even more grueling on stomachs full of tacos and enchiladas—when we heard their car roar by.

"Well, at least they didn't see us run in here," said Jon.

"How can you be so sure?" I asked, still trying to catch my breath.

"Because they sped by so fast. If they had known we were in here, they'd have stopped, I think."

"What's their beef?" I said. "You asked them a perfectly legitimate question back there at Mexico Pete's. What did you ever do to them?"

"It's not a matter of doing anything," said Jon. "Like I told you that time they first harassed us while we were walking home—I'm good with computers. None of them is. Still, they took a level-two computer course hoping to catch the eye of Miss Scaroni, who is a real knockout, as I'm sure you must have noticed when you met her on the last day of school. Miss Scaroni didn't pay any attention to them and she did pay attention to me. So . . ."

"But school's over," I protested, knowing that wasn't really the solution to anything.

"It's also a matter of those who think they're strong trying to prey on those they think are weak. If it wasn't me, it would be somebody else. They're going to show *somebody* that they're tough guys. I'm just the unlucky stiff they chose."

"Bad choice of words," I said, looking around at the gravestones surrounding us.

"Right," said Jon, the barest hint of a grin returning to his face. "We'd better stop communing with the dead and find a safe route home."

No sooner had he said that than we heard their car come roaring back up the street and once again squeal around the corner back toward Main.

"They're still on the prowl," I said.

"Do you know a back route home?" Jon asked.

"We might have to cut through a few yards," I said.

"I realize your dad wanted you home before dark, but frankly I'm glad it's getting darker," said Jon. I hadn't noticed, but the sky was getting darker by the minute.

I'm sure that if someone had been watching us from an overhead vantage point, Jon and I would have looked like something out of a cartoon as we ran from bush to bush, tree to tree, fence to fence, making our way back to Maple Street through the yards of several neighbors we have yet to meet. Several more times, we heard the car of The Four Creeps squeal its tires or gun its accelerator, but we had no close calls. We heard a police siren just about the time we reached the final dash to my front porch, so we felt safe in making our final move across the front lawn, up the steps, and into the house. (Jon had said during one of our stops that he didn't want them to discover just where I lived since he was pretty sure they didn't know my last name and wouldn't be able to track me down through the phone book.)

"Do you think the police stopped them?" I asked as we locked the door behind us.

"Part of me hopes they were the ones. Part of me hopes they weren't. It probably would only make them hate me more, since I'm sure they'd blame me for the police stopping them," said Jon.

"I hadn't thought of that," I said.

"Where have you guys been?" asked Dad, rounding the corner of the living room and trying to look like a stern father figure. "I was about to send the cops out looking for you."

"We heard their siren and decided to come home," I said, trying to sound light-hearted.

"Is everything all right?" Dad asked, concern in his voice. I guess he saw that Jon and I looked a bit rattled.

"Nothing we should talk about while Kiersten is still up," I said. "Is it OK with you if Jon stays here and watches TV with us for a while?"

"Sure," Dad said, "if he doesn't mind watching the last part of *The Sound of Music.*"

"*The Sound of Music* again?" I asked. "Kiersten has seen that at least a hundred times."

"I know. She sings along with all the songs. Actually, we've been singing duets," said Dad.

Jon and I watched the last forty-five minutes or so of *The Sound of Music*—which really is one of my favorite musicals, too. When the movie was over, Kiersten came to give me a good-night hug and said as she did, "Katelyn, would you run away to the mountains with me to escape if the bad guys were after *us?*"

"I certainly would!" I said. I couldn't help but think that the bad guys *were* after me. Unfortunately, our house was on the wrong side of the Alps!

Jon and I went into the kitchen to get cold drinks while Dad tucked Kiersten into bed. "Do you think we should tell my dad what happened?" I said.

"I don't want to worry him," said Jon. "On the other hand, I'd rather he know so he can be on the lookout for those guys should they come prowling around."

"You're probably right," I said. We really didn't have much choice because no sooner had Dad come back into the living room than he said, "OK, what gives? You guys looked like two scared rabbits when you came in that front door."

Jon and I explained what had happened, and then Jon said something that really surprised me. "On the one hand, I'd like nothing better," he said, "than to get each one of those guys alone in the boxing ring at the gym and pummel him into an unconscious state. I just don't know how to take on four guys at once."

"And on the other hand?" Dad asked.

"On the other hand, I feel guilty hating these guys so much. I don't have a Christlike attitude toward them—not even a little."

"I feel bad about that, too," I said. "I can't believe I said what I did about their being straight from hell."

"It was a great line," said Jon with a grin, "but I know what you mean."

"Well, actually," said Dad, "their attitude *is* straight from the pit. They aren't. They're just four guys who don't know who they are and who are trying to put up a tough-guy front for the world to see."

"What would you do, Mr. Weber?" Jon asked.

"I'm not real sure," said Dad. That's one thing I've always appreciated about Dad. He never tries to be something he isn't, or sound like he has all the answers. "My first impulse is to phone the police, but I'm not sure that would really do you kids any good. My second impulse is to try to find out their last names and see what I can learn about their families. Maybe I can talk to their fathers."

"That sounds a lot like the police," I said.

"You may be right, Katelyn," Dad admitted. "I suspect that the third option we have at this point is probably the one we ought to take."

"What's that?" asked Jon.

"We need to pray about and for these guys," Dad said.

Jon and I just sat there in silence for a few moments. Pray for these guys?

"Dad, I've got to admit that I'll find it very hard to pray that God will bless these guys," I finally said. Jon just nodded.

"Who said anything about asking God to *bless* them?" said Dad.

"What do you mean?" I asked.

"I had more in mind that we would pray together first that God would protect the two of you—physically and emotionally—and also protect your father, Jon, and your home, and our home here. And then I think we should turn these guys over to God and ask the Lord to deal with them in the way He wants to," said Dad.

"Now that's a prayer I can pray," said Jon.

"Not quite so fast," said Dad. "One of the things we have to recognize is that God loves those guys—as hard as that is for any of us to imagine at this moment—and that He wants them to have a real change of heart and become His followers."

"You're right, Dad," I said. "That is hard to imagine."

"Still," said Dad, "you and Jon both know that's true. Therefore . . . when we pray that God will deal with them, we are actually praying that God will turn circumstances and situations around in their lives so that they will *want* to know Jesus. If they come to Jesus, that's the best thing that can happen—not only for them, but for you two."

"I see your point," said Jon. "It's just hard to think that they'd ever turn to God."

"It would be a r-e-a-l miracle," I added.

"Well, that's the only kind I want to believe in," said Dad. "Do you think we should pray right now?"

Jon and I both nodded our heads and then we took one another's hands and Dad prayed a fantastic prayer.

I love to hear Dad pray. He really prays with boldness, as if he knows without any doubt that God is hearing him and that God is going to answer. I don't remember all that Dad said because someplace along the line, I started to cry, but I do remember that Dad prayed that God would send His angels to keep Jon and me safe, and that God would move into the lives of Dirk, Jim, Paul, and Skip with, I think Dad called it, "invasion-force power." Dad prayed that they would encounter Jesus and come to know Him as their Savior and Lord.

When he finished praying, Jon squeezed my hand and I squeezed his hand back. I think we both felt better. Then Dad volunteered to drive Jon home.

"Thanks," said Jon, "but I'll be all right. I've got angels with me, remember?"

As Jon got ready to walk out the front door, he said in a low voice to me, "Do you think Dad and Aunt Beverly had such an exciting evening?"

"I doubt it," I said with a smile. "Call me when you get home, OK?" Jon grinned and walked out the door. He phoned a couple of minutes later and I picked up the phone on the first ring so Kiersten wouldn't wake up.

"Home free," he said.

"I'm glad," I said. "Next time, let's try Tony's."

He laughed and said, "Right. We should spread the excitement around a little."

When he hung up, I thought again about Aunt Beverly and her date with Mr. Clark Weaver. I wonder what kind of time they *did* have. Maybe they should have gone to Mexico Pete's after all.

# Chapter Six

# Birthday Bash

*I*'m tired of being a day behind in my writing, dear Journal, but I'm sure you're also weary of my promising in a definitive, absolute, final manner to "catch up." I'll do the best I can, but without promises. (I'm writing during my lunch hour at the shop. It's a pretty slow day, so far.)

Sunday morning was a great service at church. The praise songs were all about God's protective power—His might, His desire that we be kept safe in His hands, His love that shields and defends. When we sang "A Mighty Fortress Is Our God," I could hardly hold back the tears. And then . . . the pastor preached on God's deliverance of Shadrach, Meshach, and Abed-Nego from Nebuchadnezzar's extra-hot furnace. I love that story in the book of

Daniel, chapter three. It's one of Kiersten's favorites, too. We have an audio tape with the story on it, complete with sound effects and music. I'll have to see if I can find it and play it again. It's been a couple of years since I heard it.

Anyway . . . I came away from the service feeling that The Four Creeps couldn't possibly be any more powerful or scary than old Nebuchadnezzar had been. And I found myself asking the Lord to give me the courage that Shadrach, Meshach, and Abed-Nego had experienced.

I caught Jon's eye twice during the service. It was as if God had arranged the song service as a confidence builder just for us.

Sunday afternoon, as you already know, I baked a cake for Dennis's party. Kimber was in charge of punch and of preparing a card we could all sign. Libby and Trish said that they'd put their heads together and provide the entertainment . . . and ice cream to go with the cake. I put out the cake—complete with sixteen candles on it—blew up a few balloons, and set out all the plates, glasses, forks, and napkins. And then I headed for youth group.

You should have seen us trying to pass Dennis's card from person to person so we could all sign it during the service—without Dennis seeing us, of course. We made it—at least as far as we know.

Dennis never let on that he had seen what we were doing.

The youth group meeting itself was a little different. Normally, Bert shares a devotional and his wife, Sharyn, leads the singing of some choruses. This night, Sharyn gave the devotional. Actually, it was her personal testimony. She told how she had grown up in a preacher's home, but had become a really rebellious teen-ager. I can't put down word for word everything she said, but I do remember this part: She said, "I really wanted to win a certain award that was given in our school—it meant a chance to travel across the state and be part of a very elite student choir. I prayed about getting the award and was just sure that God was going to let me win. When the announcement was made, however, my name wasn't the one that was called! I was named runner-up, which meant a long hot summer at home, while a girl I didn't like very much got to travel around the state and have a great time. I felt God had really let me down, so I decided that He would no longer be my Friend. Basically, I was mad at God. What I didn't realize was that God doesn't exist to do what *we* want Him to do. We were created to do what *He* wants *us* to do. It was only years later that I realized that if I had gone on that choir trip, I wouldn't have met Bert. So you see, God had a better plan in motion all along."

While Sharyn was speaking, I wanted to glance at Trish to see how she was responding to Sharyn's words, but I didn't dare since she was sitting right next to me. I was just glad that Trish was there. She hasn't wanted to come to youth group and probably wouldn't have come last night if we hadn't planned the special party for Dennis.

Anyway . . . after the service, Dennis offered to drive us all home and by "advance planning," Julio suggested that he drop me off first. When we got to the house, Jon said that he wanted to come in to get something that he had mistakenly left at my house. Actually, that wasn't a lie. Jon had forgotten to take home the two extra boxes of dye we didn't use when we did his T-shirts. So . . . once Jon was in the house, we turned off all the lights.

That, of course, led to all kinds of speculation in the car—or so Libby told me later. "I thought they said they were just *friends*," said Julio. "Do you think they were mugged?" asked Trish. Dennis, of course, didn't have a clue as to what was going on, so he really fell for the plot we had concocted. He finally said, "I think we should go check," and he led the entire gang up to the front porch in hot pursuit of Jon. As soon as he knocked on the door, Jon and I opened the door, turned on the lights, and started singing "Happy Birthday." Jon and I had lit the candles on the cake in a big hurry and I was standing there holding the blazing cake as Jon opened the door.

"Surprise!" everybody shouted after we finished the song. Dennis was!

In fact, he seemed truly and genuinely stunned. He came to, though, when he was asked how big a piece of cake he wanted.

"You mean that isn't *my* piece?" he said, gesturing at the entire cake.

"Not if you want any friends for the summer," said Julio as he reached over to scoop up a bit of frosting with his little finger. "If you be wanting friends, you'd best be letting 'em share your cake," he added, in an accent that sounded decisively more Irish than Indian. "Kinda slipped there," admitted Julio.

In spite of the short notice, we had managed to come up with a few gifts for Dennis. Julio and Jon had gone together to give him a free tennis lesson at the Collinsville Family Fitness Center. Libby, Trish, and I gave him a key chain with a big "D" on it—an item that Grandpa Stone brought to me from the hardware store on his way home from church. (He said he had felt like he was breaking into his own store, since he didn't recall ever being inside the store on a Sunday afternoon. Stone's Hardware is closed on Sundays, like most of the businesses in the downtown district, and unlike most of the businesses in the rest of the town.)

We also gave him a hot-rod model kit, as a gag gift. "It's your new car," we said, knowing full well that Dennis is going to be stuck driving his family's Chevrolet for a couple of years.

Kimber gave Dennis a little painting that she had done of a boy fishing off the end of a dock. Dennis loves to fish and talks about it all the time. He's even trying to work in a fishing stop or two on our big bike trip.

Kimber's painting also had weeping willow trees in it and a couple of ducks waddling toward the pond. It was really *good*. I could tell Dennis was very pleased. Kimber told me later that she thinks it's the best painting she's ever done. "The best for the best," I said.

"That's what I thought, too," she said with a smile.

And then, after Dennis had opened his gifts, Libby and Trish announced that they had a special song just for him. Libby pulled out a kazoo—which caused all of us to laugh even before she had made a sound. Libby and a kazoo just don't seem to go together . . . at all! "What were you all l-l-l-laughing about?" she asked me later.

"You and a kazoo?" I said. "I can imagine you with just about any instrument *other* than a kazoo. It just isn't you, Libby. Or at least we didn't *think* so."

"Even stutterers can h-h-h-hum a kazoo tune,"

she said with a laugh. I'm really glad Libby is able to laugh more around us, including laughing at her own stuttering. I think that's a sign of real inner strength.

Anyway . . . the song itself was also a hoot. Trish sang and mimicked her way through the lyrics that she and Libby had pulled together—all about Dennis, the bike man . . . Dennis, the fisherman . . . Dennis, the all-around man's man . . . Dennis, the over-the-hill man at sixteen. It was a real roast, but Dennis took it well. He laughed as hard as the rest of us as Trish acted out his various mannerisms and the way he talks.

I was amazed at Trish's acting ability. And Libby's song-writing ability. They make quite a team! "Webster and Martin." It has a ring to it!

At the end of the song, Trish said, "And now, Dennis, you'll have to pucker up, because we don't want you to be sweet sixteen and never been kissed!"

I was absolutely floored. This was *not* a part of our plans! Trish immediately bounced over to Dennis and planted a great big kiss right on his mouth and then said, to my utter shock . . . the greatest shock of my life . . . well, at least of the month . . . "Your turn, Katelyn!"

I guess a bolt of sheer madness must have struck me because I did just what Trish had done—I swooned into Dennis's arms and gave him a big kiss too, and said, "Your turn, Libby." She flounced over and kissed Dennis—I think she was more surprised than Dennis was! And that left . . . Kimber.

For us, of course, all of this couldn't really be counted as kissing. I'm still fourteen and three-quarters and have never been kissed . . . at least as far as I'm concerned. Zeb Neeley of Eagle Rock might have a different opinion, but his stolen kiss on a roller-coaster ride wasn't something that I was choosing to participate in . . . just as Dennis wasn't choosing to have us girls kiss him. That's what matters I think, in a *real* kiss. Both people in a real kiss have to want the kiss and be equal partners in it.

Which, of course, is exactly the position that Kimber and Dennis were in! I really felt bad for Kimber but she pretended it was all a joke, just as we had, and she sat down on Dennis's knee and after pushing up the sleeves on her blouse as if she was really getting ready to go to work, she gave him a loud smacker. Unfortunately for her, Dennis didn't let go! He kissed her back! Which got everybody laughing, except Kimber, of course. She turned red as a beet, which is something I didn't know Chinese girls could do. (She reminded me later that she's only *half* Chinese.)

"Take it outside, you two," said Trish. And Dennis did just that. He started to lead Kimber away by the arm, but Julio saved the day by saying, "No way. If they leave together, the rest of us will never get home."

That broke up the party. Everybody—except Jon—climbed back into the Andersons' Chevrolet and drove away. I talked to Kimber today and unfortunately for her, her stop was next so she didn't get a chance to give Dennis the "real" kiss she had hoped they'd share. She had a pretty good attitude about it, though. "The entire summer is ahead of us!" she said.

Jon helped me clean up the kitchen after everybody left. Dad came downstairs to get a piece of cake. "That service this morning was really for you kids, wasn't it?" he said.

"Yeah, it was as if God really has our number," said Jon. "I even found myself praying for those guys this afternoon—not only that they'd stay away from Katelyn, but that they'd become Christians. I'm glad you said what you did last night."

"I've been praying, too," said Dad as he went back upstairs with his cake. "Lock the door when Jon leaves, OK, Kat-Kat?" Dad reminded me.

"Kat-Kat?" Jon said, with a teasing grin.

"Everybody has a nickname," I said, with an equal tease in my voice. "Some nicknames are just better than others."

"I wish I were sixteen," Jon said, a real gleam in his eye.

"Well, you're *n-o-t*," I said and pushed him toward the door.

One kiss a night is enough for any fourteen-year-old. The fact is, I might have *wanted* to be part of a kiss with Jon and that is a really scary thought. Friends just don't kiss. At least not for *real*.

# Chapter Seven

# The First Bike Ride

**Thursday**
**10 P.M.**

$\mathcal{B}$oy, am I pooped.

Actually, I don't assume, dear Journal, that you are a boy. Or a girl, for that matter. The fact is, I'm so tired I'm feeling punchy.

The FF Club met on Tuesday as planned, and part of our business meeting was devoted to planning our bike-ride schedule. We decided to have seven rides over a three-week period in order to build ourselves up to an all-day ride to Benton, which we scheduled for two weeks from this coming Saturday. Both Grandpa Stone and Dad have said they'll pick us up in Benton at the end of the ride and drive us back to Collinsville.

I was really pleased that everybody who had something to do for the meeting came prepared.

Jon and Dennis brought maps and they had already drawn out the six short routes—each just a little bit longer than the previous ride. All of the rides are around Collinsville except for one that goes out into River Gorge. We planned rides for Tuesday and Thursday evenings, and Saturday mornings.

I told the club that Grandpa Stone has agreed to loan us the litter spears and is also going to donate the trash bags to our club. Kimber commented, "That's a lot cheaper than any price I got," which brought a laugh from everybody. I also shared the great news that Grandpa Stone is also willing to pay for our T-shirts if we will wear Stone's Hardware baseball-style caps while we are picking up litter. (At other times, Grandpa is happy for us to wear any caps we want, including our bike helmets. Grandpa's giving us the T-shirts and trash bags will really save us some money.)

That brought up the matter of T-shirts, and Kimber showed us a really neat design that she's created for the shirts. We all liked her design a lot and voted for it unanimously as our official logo.

Trish reported that she found a place that will screen-print the shirts for four dollars each for small, medium, and large, and five dollars for extra-large. We all agreed to go ahead with the shirts as quickly as possible, and that we would be happy to wear Stone's Hardware caps while we're picking up trash. Libby made a list of the sizes we want to order: one medium, three large, and three extra-large.

Jon said that his dad had offered to give each bike rider a free water bottle with the Collinsville Family Fitness Center name on it. Thank you, Mr. Clark Weaver! (Julio quipped that if we worked the club right, we might get corporate sponsorship for everything, and that he would be happy to volunteer as our television commercial spokesman . . . "for the right fee." Yeah, sure, Julio.) Julio is also letting Trish borrow his old bike since he just got a new one.

Libby suggested that we have picnics on Saturdays only and just bring along snack bars for the rides on Tuesday and Thursday nights—granola bars, candy bars, whatever. We figured that was a smart idea since we'll be riding after dinner on Tuesdays and Thursdays. She signed everybody up for things to bring using a really unusual method. Libby always seems to have clever ideas! She had a set of Popsicle sticks on which she had written words like "sandwiches," "potato chips," "soft drinks," and so forth. Then she held the sticks so we only saw the tips and not the words. We each drew a stick and that is what we are to bring for this Saturday's ride. I'm supposed to bring a sandwich for each person, and so is Kimber. We decided we'd get together on Friday night to make the sandwich fillings, and then meet a half hour early on Saturday morning to make the sandwiches.

Julio showed us his bike-repair kit and we all looked at the different tools and items in it. Libby suggested that one of us also bring along a first-aid kit, just in case somebody had an accident. Another good Libby idea. Julio offered to help anybody who needed bike repairs on Wednesday night.

Trish and I decided to take our bicycles over to have them checked out. It's a good thing we did. Julio found a deep thorn stuck into my rear tire and he suggested that I have it removed and the tire officially patched before the ride. When I told Dad about it, he suggested that I should just get two new tires for the bike and that he was willing to pay for them—so I spent my lunch hour today at Collinsville Cycle—a bicycle and motorcycle shop in town—getting new tires. Trish's bike was in good order. Julio did show her how to use the gears. She had never ridden a bicycle with gears before.

Getting back to our FF meeting on Tuesday, the last part of the hour we got down to the serious business of going over the bicycle routes that Jon and Dennis had mapped out. We all decided that they had done a great job of mapping out the sequence of routes to take, allowing us to cover a big percentage of the streets in central Collinsville on our "litter patrol," and we decided to meet at seven o'clock this evening for our first ride. Which is what we did.

We met at Jon's house. Grandpa Stone surprised me by showing up with our T-shirts, so we were a little bit delayed in getting started because we all wanted to change into them right away. (Except for Kimber, who bemoaned the fact that the red and brown shirt clashed with her orange and yellow shorts. She was a good sport about it, though, and wore the T-shirt.) Grandpa Stone also brought the caps, litter spears, and trash bags. It was kinda exciting—it seemed like we were all dressing up for a major event.

After the meeting on Tuesday, Jon and I had discussed on the phone the possibility of our starting each meeting and each bike ride with a brief little prayer. I thought that was a great idea, and frankly, I was a little upset at myself for not thinking of it first.

"Why didn't you bring it up at the meeting?" I asked him.

"I thought I should talk to you about it first. After all, you're the prez," he said.

"Sure," I said, knowing he was teasing me. "Well, Mr. Vice-Prez, feel free to introduce good ideas like that any time!"

So . . . before we started the ride, I shared with the group Jon's idea and everybody thought it was fine—at least nobody protested—so Jon said a brief prayer before we started out. And by 7:30 we hit the trail!

We only rode for four miles. But . . . one of the things we realized very quickly was that Jon and Dennis had been dealing with a flat map—and Collinsville is anything but flat! They hadn't—and none of us had—counted on the hills.

It took us a full hour to cover the four miles, by the time we walked our bikes up a couple of hills and stopped to rest a couple of times. Not to mention the occasional stop to pick up trash.

For the most part, the central part of Collinsville is pretty free of litter. We did find a couple of patches that were pretty bad—it looked as if maybe the wind had blown the trash together by a fence on Myrtle Street. Generally speaking, the guys did most of the litter spearing. They turned the litter gathering into a game of sorts—seeing who could ride to a piece of litter and spear it without getting off his bike. Actually, I think they were showing off a bit for the benefit of us girls. I did notice, however, that by the last half of the ride, they were more subdued. Dennis even commented, "This litter spearing is a lot like work!"

One of the things we did discover is that not all litter is spearable. That really became evident as we tried to clean up the patch of litter on Myrtle Street. We agreed that in the future, we each need to bring along work gloves of some type. The word "germs" took on a whole new meaning.

While we were cleaning up the mess there—which included lots of bottles and empty beer cans, Libby said, "I didn't know we'd be d-d-d-dealing with a t-t-t-toxic dump!" That became the joke of the evening. Anytime we saw a patch of litter, one of us would call out, "Toxic dump alert!" I'm not sure what the neighbors in that part of town must have thought!

In all, we picked up nearly two full trash bags of litter—by the time we emptied our partial sacks together.

Anyway, we returned to Jon's house about 8:45 to find that Jon's dad had whipped up some home-made ice cream. That was a real treat. None of us had remembered to bring along candy or granola bars, although we all returned home with pretty empty water bottles. The ice cream had bits of peanut brittle in it. And . . . guess who else was there? Aunt Beverly! She had never met Dennis, Libby, or Julio, so there were lots of introductions all around. Apparently the peanut brittle was Aunt Beverly's idea. A really good one, as far as I was concerned!

I've got to tease Aunt Beverly a little when I see her at the shop in the morning. Actually, I've been teasing her all week.

I could hardly wait to get to The Wonderful

Life Shop on Monday morning to see how her date had gone. (She went with Grandpa Stone to church on Sunday and we didn't see her Sunday afternoon or evening.)

"Good," she said with a smile.

"Is that *all* you're going to say about it?" I said.

"It was good," she repeated.

I know you're probably going to find this difficult to believe, but I think that's the first time Aunt Beverly has said that an evening was "good" without qualifying it in some way. Usually she has a funny story to tell, or she will describe some really quirky thing the guy did or said. I didn't know quite what to do with a description of just "good."

"Well, tell me about dinner," I said.

"We went to a little place called Chez José," she said.

"So what's that?" I asked. "French or Spanish?"

"A little of both, I think," Aunt Beverly explained. "And mostly just plain delicious." She went on to explain, "The menu had only five items on it, and they all sounded wonderful. Plus a few other odds and ends as side dishes and starters."

"So what did you have?" I asked. If she wasn't going to tell me about Mr. Clark Weaver, I could at least get her to describe the food.

"I had a cup of the baked potato soup to start with," she said.

*"Baked potato soup?"* I asked.

"Yes, it was really delicious. It was basically cream of potato soup with cheese added, and then, on top, it was garnished with a little sour cream, some bacon bits, and a few chives."

"Sounds yummy."

"It was. And then I had a Caesar salad with grilled chicken strips. The chicken had been marinated in something wonderful. Clark had a small regular Caesar salad and an entrée—pork chops with an apple and cranberry chutney, and a delicious spinach soufflé and potatoes *au gratin* on the side. He had their vegetable soup instead of the baked potato soup."

"It's really a gourmet place," I said, and thinking back to *my* tacos on Saturday night, I added, "Definitely a notch or two above Mexico Pete's."

"I *like* Mexico Pete's," Aunt Beverly said. "You always give that place a hard time."

"Wait till you hear what happened to Jon and me there."

"What?" she asked.

"I want to hear about dessert first."

"Oh, that was wonderful. It's why I had just a salad for dinner. They had the most incredible chocolate dessert—he called it 'chocolate pâté'— like a very heavy mousse, I guess. Underneath it were two sauces, each covering half the plate—a white chocolate sauce and a raspberry sauce."

"Heavenly," I said.

"Exactly."

"Did you go anyplace afterwards?" I asked.

"We really didn't need to. Chez José's has a great little jazz combo that plays there on Friday and Saturday nights—we stayed and listened to the music over coffee for a couple of hours. And then we came home."

"Did he kiss you?" I teased.

"No, he didn't," she said. "We were too busy laughing."

"He's fun to be with, then?" I asked.

"Very. I don't know how your friendship is with Jon, but his father is *very* easy to talk to, and is very witty."

"That's Jon," I said. "He's as easy to talk to as any girlfriend I've ever had."

"That's the way it is with Clark, too," Aunt Beverly said. "I think we're going to be very good friends."

"Is that all?" I teased.

"That's a pretty good start," she said.

"But is that *all* you want your relationship to be with him?" I pressed.

"I don't know, Katelyn," Aunt Beverly said. She had a whimsical tone to her voice. "Maybe not. We'll see what grows." That's such an Aunt Beverly statement—"We'll see what grows." She's always into things taking time. I'm into instant results!

I couldn't get much more out of Aunt Beverly about Saturday night but I've finally decided, dear Journal, that "good" is probably "very good" in anybody else's book. Aunt Beverly isn't one to exaggerate.

Aunt Beverly, of course, really grilled me for all the details about what happened Saturday night. She was very concerned. "This could be dangerous," she said. "If I were you, Katelyn, I'd do everything possible to avoid those boys."

"We didn't exactly go looking for them," I said. "And we can't stay locked up indoors all summer."

"No, I guess you're right," she said. "I just don't like the sound of it. They are the kind of guys that become the ringleaders of gangs, and that's the *last* thing we need in Collinsville."

I told her about Dad's prayer, and Aunt Beverly said, "Well, I'll certainly be praying for you, too." The way she said it, I knew she'd not only be praying hard but that she was probably also going to try to talk to Dad about what had happened.

On the one hand, I'm sorry I told her about the incident because I don't want her to worry. On the other hand, I'm glad she knows so she can pray— and also because I just don't like having secrets from Aunt Beverly.

Then again, she has a couple of secrets she's keeping from me! For one, I had no idea she was planning to go over to Mr. Clark Weaver's to help him fix peanut-brittle ice cream for us on Thursday night.

Right before I came home tonight, Jon said to Aunt Beverly, "I'm expecting another shipment from Grandma Turner tomorrow or the next day. Want to help me evaluate it?"

"Sure," Aunt Beverly said. "Now that you're looking so sharp, we can't afford any relapses!"

It will be fun to see what Grandma Turner sends. For now, dear Journal, I must say good night. And, I trust you realize, I'm finally caught up in telling you everything that is going on. It's taken me a while, I know, and I'll try not to let that happen again. I really *don't* like loose ends!

# Chapter Eight

# Confidences

Friday
7 P.M.

*F*amous last words. I just caught up telling you everything, dear Journal, and now here it is, eight whole days later!

I have some major things to report, though. Life has been busy in Collinsville—with a whole lot of bike riding going on! I'll *try* to take things in sequence. . . .

On Friday afternoon, Jon called the shop to say that, indeed, a packet had arrived from Grandma Turner, so on our way home from the shop, Aunt Beverly and I stopped to see what she had sent. Actually, this packet was pretty cool. She had sent two wide-striped T-shirts, a navy nylon windbreaker, and a pair of navy shorts.

"Did you tell her that you changed your look?" I asked.

"No," said Jon, "I haven't said a thing. Dad did take some pictures, though, last week. He might have sent one to her, but I'm not sure she would have received it before she sent this packet."

"Whatever," said Aunt Beverly. "These clothes are all very much in fashion."

"Pictures?" I said. "Can I see what your dad took?"

"OK," said Jon as he rummaged through a stack of stuff on the kitchen counter—which is where we had gone to open the box of clothes.

"Your dad is a really good photographer," I said.

"It's his hobby," Jon said. "Dad is really into camera gear and taking nature photographs. He said these were for 'Christmas gifts' for the relatives."

"Christmas? It's still June," I said.

"Yeah, I know," said Jon. "I think that was just an excuse to try out a new camera he just purchased. Dad always figures you should take lots of photos and well in advance so you can reshoot whatever you might want to. He's always trying to get just the right lighting and poses."

"You're a good model," I said.

"Well, I've been his guinea pig for nearly fifteen years," Jon laughed.

"I'm serious," I said. "You are very photogenic."

"It's something you learn to be, I think," Jon replied. "Like everything—practice makes perfect." Overall, he didn't seem to think the photos were any big deal.

I, on the other hand, was thoroughly impressed. Mr. Clark Weaver had managed to get Jon to pose—apparently by the trees in their backyard—for quite a few shots, and in several different outfits. Some close-ups, some showing his full height. Nearly every photo was a good one.

Aunt Beverly and I laid them all out on the kitchen counter and pored over them for a few minutes. I knew Aunt Beverly's mind was spinning, but I had no idea what she was thinking.

"What are the chances of my taking one of these?" I asked.

"Pick out whatever you want," said Jon. He was still being s-o-o-o-o casual about this. "Dad's got the negatives, and he nearly always orders enlargements of the ones he wants to send as gifts to my aunts and grandmothers."

I picked out three great shots, and tucked them into my purse. Aunt Beverly then asked, "Can I just borrow the rest of these for a little bit?"

"I don't see why not," Jon said. "It might be a good idea to leave behind the negatives, though. Dad has this thing about negatives walking out of the house."

"Fine," said Aunt Beverly as she separated the prints from the packet of negatives. "I'll only keep

**98**

them a few days." I still had no idea what she had up her sleeve.

About that time, Mr. Clark Weaver walked in and suggested that we all go to Porter's Restaurant for dinner. I called Dad and Kiersten and they said that suited them just fine—they'd meet us there. Even Grandpa decided to come along. It wasn't as if we didn't have dinner at home. Mrs. Miller had made a fabulous pan of lasagna. Still, we knew we could have that on Saturday. So . . . we all converged on Porter's for dinner, eight of us in all since Mari came along with Kiersten.

It was a fun time. I think that's the first time Dad and Mr. Clark Weaver have had a chance to talk, and they really seemed to hit it off. Aunt Beverly seemed pleased. It was also the first time that Jon had met Mari, or had much time to spend with Kiersten. He was really nice to the two twerps. They got to talking in Pig Latin, which, come to find out, Jon is very fluent in speaking! "It's my best foreign language," he said. Kiersti was impressed.

On Saturday, I helped out at the shop. Aunt Beverly received a huge shipment of new things—including some very clever teapots and some pretty floral place mats and napkins. She also got in a big new selection of blank books, so—I hope this doesn't upset you, dear Journal—I chose my next book to write in. It's covered with fabric that has big, bold, hot-pink dahlias against a black background. Normally I'm not a floral person, but this cover is definitely, as Aunt Beverly said, "high drama."

On Saturday—promptly at five o'clock in the afternoon—we took our second bike ride. I was still a little sore from the first trip. In fact, when I got up on Friday morning, I didn't see how I could possibly ride on Saturday . . . and perhaps not ever! I discovered some muscles I didn't know I had! My legs felt better on Saturday, and fortunately, Jon and Dennis had mapped out a flatter route this time. They admitted they hadn't taken any hills into consideration when they did their first set of maps, but this time they kept us mostly on flat terrain. If they hadn't altered the route, I'm not sure Libby would have gone. She was *really* sore after the first ride.

We only picked up one full bag of trash. The neighborhoods we rode through were pretty clean. The same for Thursday night. But . . . I'm getting ahead of myself.

After the ride on Saturday—complete with a picnic stop at the park next to the high school— Libby came over to my house for a few minutes to talk. She had been very quiet on the ride and I could tell something was bothering her.

"What's up?" I asked as we plopped down on the porch.

"It's my m-m-m-mother," she said.

"Your mom?" I said. "What's wrong with her?"

"It's not her, exactly," said Libby. "It's our relationship. We just can't seem to c-c-c-communicate."

"Oh, Libby," I said, "surely it isn't all that bad."

"But it is," she said. "I don't even like to t-t-t-talk to you about this since your mom isn't here. But my mother is so r-r-r-remote she might as well be dead."

"Libby, don't say that!" I said. "As long as your mother *is* alive, there's hope that things can improve. What exactly does she say to you?"

"Th-th-th-that's just it," Libby said. "She doesn't say very much at all. Most of the time she talks to my b-b-b-brothers, Mick and David. Everything she does seems to revolve around them. My father and I get pushed to the side all the time. It's M-m-m-mick needs this, or David that. They always come first."

"Can you talk to your dad about this?"

"Dad's real quiet. He just sticks his nose in the p-p-p-paper and ignores Mom most of the t-t-t-time," said Libby. "When Mom does talk to m-m-m-me, it's usually to tell me that I'm doing something that she d-d-d-doesn't approve of," she said.

"Like what?" I said. I couldn't think of anything that Libby would do that would be unaccept-able to my dad or to Aunt Beverly.

"She doesn't like the way I d-d-d-dress, for one thing," said Libby, and by this time I could see big silent tears beginning to form in her eyes.

"But you dress great," I said. "You always look so colorful and relaxed. It's summer. What does your mom want you to wear?"

"Mom's into high heels and s-s-s-suits," said Libby. "Very t-t-t-tailored."

"So, you have a different look," I said.

"She's also very p-p-p-petite," said Libby. "She's always after me to l-l-l-lose a few pounds."

"But maybe you're not built like your mother," I said. "Not everybody can be a skinny-minny . . . or should be!"

"We're not built at all alike. I'm more like my f-f-f-father's family," said Libby. And then she added, "But that's not the worst thing."

"What more is there?" I asked. It seemed to me that Libby's mother already had a full plate of dislikes.

"My mother wants me to stay home and not ride b-b-b-bikes with you and the others in the c-c-c-club," said Libby. At that, the tears that had puddled in her eyes began to trickle down her cheeks like two shiny stripes.

"No way!" I said. "Do you want me to go talk to her?"

"I don't think it would help," Libby said. "She thinks riding bicycles at my age is too un-l-l-l-ladylike."

"Well, we never claimed to be *ladies*," I teased, trying to get a smile out of Libby. I succeeded, but barely.

"Mom doesn't know I went r-r-r-riding to-night," said Libby. "That's why I asked if I could come over to your house to change c-c-c-clothes."

"I wondered about that," I said. "Well, for now I hope you'll continue to ride with us—at least until we can figure out what to do about this."

"There's nothing *to* do," said Libby with a giant sigh.

"Did your mother say specifically that you *can't* ride with us, or that she just disapproves?" I asked Libby. I know that it's wrong for Libby to disobey her mother, but if her mother hadn't actually said that Libby *couldn't* ride, that didn't seem the same to me as if she had said that Libby *shouldn't* ride.

"I don't really know," said Libby. "We got into such an argument over it. And you know, when I get upset, I s-s-s-stutter even more."

"Let me give this a think," I said. "Why don't you park your bike here for now." That seemed like a good idea to Libby, so we rolled her bicycle into the garage next to mine, and she headed home.

"Hurry," I said, "and call me the minute you get home. It's almost dark." Libby made it home OK, but I could hardly get to sleep Saturday night. What Libby had shared with me really bothered me.

Sunday morning was church and on Sunday night, youth group was canceled. Pastor Bert and Sharyn had to go out of town unexpectedly because Sharyn's grandfather had a heart attack. We prayed for him in church on Sunday morning.

Since there was no youth group, Jon came down to the house just to hang out and talk. I hadn't talked to him much during either of our bike rides, so it felt good to catch up a little with him.

As it started to get dark, Jon said, "I keep thinking about what happened at Mexico Pete's."

"I do too," I admitted. "There are lots of different angles to think about."

"One of the things those guys said has really bothered me," said Jon.

"What?" I asked.

"The part where they said that my new look couldn't change me from being a nerd," said Jon, barely above a whisper. It was the first time that Jon has ever seemed the least bit embarrassed to say something to me. He definitely wasn't grinning.

"Oh, they were just jealous," I said.

"Maybe," said Jon. "But it felt more like the truth to me."

"But, Jon," I said, "you never were a nerd. *You've* called yourself a nerd, but nobody else I know thinks of you that way. So you like computers and you're good at math. That's not the total you!"

"But sometimes I feel as if that *is* the total me," said Jon.

"You work out at the gym," I said.

"Yes, but I'm not into sports," said Jon. "Not really—not like Dennis is. I don't know all the statistics about the professional teams, and I've never played very much baseball or football. And I'm not into mechanical things or cars or music, like Julio is."

"So?" I said, trying to figure out what more I could say to help Jon see that he is anything but a nerd in *my* book.

"Sometimes when I look at myself in the mirror these past couple of weeks, I find myself saying out loud, 'Who is that guy?' It just doesn't feel like me. The guy in the mirror doesn't look like a nerd, but the guy sitting here on the porch by you *feels* like a nerd. Dirk is right."

"No, he's not," I said, feeling a rising sense of indignation. "Dirk most definitely is *not* right. He was just saying that to put you down, and I won't let you buy what he said as being the truth. You can look any way you want to look. It isn't a matter of being a nerd or not being a nerd. It's a matter of looking a way that makes you feel good about yourself. It takes time to get used to a new look. In fact, I'm just now getting to where I really feel comfortable with my hair this length. You'll get used to your new look, if you want to get used to it." I was so upset that I knew I was talking too fast. I probably didn't make much sense to Jon.

"The difference, Katelyn," said Jon, "is that you're confident inside yourself about who you are. No matter how you look on the outside, you have been the same on the inside—a positive, pretty confident . . . *woman!* Your new outward appearance just matches the way you always were on the inside. Me? I'm also the same on the inside, even though the outside of me has changed. The difference is, the *old* outside matched my inside. The new outside doesn't!"

"So what now?" I said. "Do you want to go back to the old look?"

"No," said Jon, but not very strongly.

"If that's what you want, Jon, it's fine with me," I said. "I'll like you and be your friend either way. It doesn't matter to me. If you're more comfortable with your old haircut, glasses, and button-down shirts, that's OK. I'm not sure what we can do about un-dying those T-shirts, however. You may

**106**

have to wait for Grandma Turner to send you some more white ones."

Jon grimaced, and *almost* grinned.

"That's not what I want," said Jon. "What I really want, Katelyn, is to change the *inside* of me to match the new outside."

"What about your inside don't you like?" I asked. I knew from our conversation a few weeks ago that Jon knew the Lord Jesus as his personal Savior and Lord, so it wasn't that kind of change that he needed in his life.

"I'm not really sure," said Jon.

"Well, when you figure it out, I'll try to be here for you as your friend, to help you any way I can, Jon Weaver," I said. And I really meant it. I reached over to touch Jon's arm and he took my hand in both of his, and then pulled my hand up to his lips and kissed the back of my hand very sweetly.

"You really are the best friend I've got," he said. And then he stood up and said, "Well, I'd better get home before the Father Patrol starts looking for me."

And that, dear Journal, isn't all.

Monday was my off day from the shop. Dad took off, too, and he and Kiersten and I drove all the way to Kidderville—which is about fifty miles beyond Benton—to see a double-header baseball game. It was lots of fun, and it felt really good for the three of us to be doing something together.

Since we moved to Collinsville earlier in the spring, we really haven't done that many things that involved just Dad, Kiersti, and me. It seems one of us has always been missing, or somebody else has always been around. Mrs. Miller also had the day off—it was her birthday—and that was probably part of the reason that Dad decided we needed an outing together. Plus, Grandpa Stone has season tickets to the games. Plus, these were two of Dad's favorite teams.

We didn't get home until late, which kept me from writing about the weekend events. In fact, it was so late that I had a hard time getting up on Tuesday and I almost was late for work.

Tuesday night was our bike ride. It's getting a little easier all the time. This time the route had a few more hills, but none of us were huffing and puffing quite as much as we did the first night. I was glad Libby came. I still haven't figured out what we can do to convince her mother that the FF Club bike rides are a good thing.

On Wednesday, I had a fun experience with Aunt Beverly. We closed the shop at noon and met at the Manor House with several other merchants in town. I realized when we got there that Aunt Beverly had called together this gathering of various shop owners. She was definitely the hostess of the hour.

The people present included Mr. McGreggor,

Grandpa Stone; Mr. DeVries—who is the manager of the Manor House; Mrs. Sally Warren—the owner of the Collinsville Inn, which is a large old stone inn in River Gorge, situated right on the river; Mr. Winters—who owns the big Amazing Antiques store where Main Street turns into East Valley Road; and Miss Jones, the owner of several of the downtown buildings. The Jones family was among the first families to settle the town. Miss Jones is in her seventies now—about ten years older than Mr. McGreggor and Grandpa Stone—but she's still a real community leader.

After we had all shared a delicious crab salad for lunch, Aunt Beverly shared some of her thoughts with the other merchants. It seems that Aunt Beverly has been thinking a lot about that day when we had the busload of tourists come into the store. "Why not go after the tourist trade?" she asked. "We all drive to Benton to shop. Why not give Bentonites a reason to drive out to Collinsville?"

"What do you have in mind, Beverly?" asked Mrs. Warren, who is a very "stately" woman, as Gramma Weber would say. She always has her gray hair in an upswept coiffure that is truly elegant. She's probably in her fifties, but she doesn't have a wrinkle on her face. She's what Mom would have called a "classic beauty," and she always seems like such a gracious hostess. Mom used to love to go to the Collinsville Inn for tea when we would come to Collinsville for visits. She'd let Kiersti and me swing on the tire that hung from the big old oak tree on the grassy slope behind the inn. That gave her some time to talk with her friends, no doubt.

"I'm not a hundred percent sure," said Aunt Beverly. "I would just like for us—as some of the foremost merchants in town—to give some thought to the idea. I think we could really develop our town into a stopover place for tourist buses. We are oozing with charm—at least, that's what outsiders say about us—even though we're so used to the way we live that we don't seem to recognize what all we have here."

"I think you're exactly right, Beverly," said Mr. McGreggor. "People are always commenting on how old-fashioned my store is. I took offense at that for a couple of years until it dawned on me that they were meaning it as a compliment. It seems some folks have never been in an old-fashioned drug store, or had a good old-fashioned soda." Just the thought of Mr. McGreggor's shop made me long to have one of his chocolate sodas for dessert.

"We could use some more guests at the Manor House," said Mr. DeVries. "Summer is a busy time for us because of weddings and honeymoons and

**110**

vacations, but we don't have much traffic after Labor Day."

"Let's think about our assets," said Aunt Beverly. "We're easily accessible—just four miles off Highway 139. In fact Highway 9 makes a detour that tourists could take and still get back on Highway 139 easily, in either direction. We're really only a mile or two extra on somebody's itinerary. We have wonderful places to spend the night and to eat. Good places to shop."

"We might need to come up with an attraction or two," said Grandpa Stone. "Maybe a farmers market on Saturday morning in the main plaza, or a sidewalk sale every Saturday."

"That's right, Mr. Stone," said Aunt Beverly. "Both of those are great ideas. And they're things that a smaller town can offer that Benton doesn't have."

"There's not much to do here at night," said Mr. Winters.

"Well, we might just have to create something to do at night," said Miss Jones. "I'm not sure the townspeople have ever given much thought to that. If we all thought about it, we might just come up with an idea or two worth pursuing."

"Overall, it means developing a general theme about how we want our town to be perceived," said Aunt Beverly. "We know that we're friendly and hard-working people. But are we a farmtown, an antiques and gift center, a river-side retreat, a quaint village . . . ?"

"How do you suggest we go about this?" said Mr. DeVries. "I think you're really onto something and I think we should pursue this."

"Well, how about our meeting for lunch every couple of weeks to see what we can come up with?" said Aunt Beverly. "Perhaps we could alternate between the Collinsville Inn and the Manor House." At that, both Mrs. Warren and Mr. DeVries nodded. "Why don't we meet two weeks from now? And maybe we could all focus our ideas on what we'd like to see done to develop ourselves for more tourist trade by next summer."

Everybody agreed and I really felt, dear Journal, as if I was at a historic meeting. It felt like the start of something new! A little like the FF Club, only more grown up. Speaking of which, while we were eating lunch, Aunt Beverly asked me to tell the group gathered there about our club. They all were very supportive. Mr. Winters said that he'd be happy to help us sponsor something, if we'd come by and talk it over with him.

As the meeting broke up, Aunt Beverly stopped to talk with Miss Jones for a few minutes. "Miss Jones," she said, "I'd like to talk to you about a couple of your empty retail properties."

"Sure thing, dear," said Miss Jones. "I can't

stand for Collinsville to have empty downtown buildings. When would you like to meet?"

"Oh, at your convenience," said Aunt Beverly. "What would be a good time and place for you?"

"Well, why don't you come by to see me at my home next Monday afternoon after you close the shop, say about five o'clock. We can have a late tea."

"Great," said Aunt Beverly. "See you then."

Once we were outside, I grabbed Aunt Beverly. "What are you thinking about doing?" I just *knew* she had something up her sleeve besides her arm. (That's a phrase Dad uses a lot. It makes me laugh every time I say it or write it!)

"Well," said Aunt Beverly, "I have just the beginnings of an idea. When I saw those great pictures of Jon, I started thinking—downtown Collinsville doesn't have a good men's shop. Nothing that is for men what Clara's is for women. And then last week I had dinner with a friend of mine who is a buyer for Norton's. She shared with me that her dream is to open up a menswear shop. She just isn't sure, given her recent divorce, whether a bank will give her the loan."

"So you're thinking of loaning her the money so she can open up a men's shop in Collinsville!" I said.

"Yes, something like that," said Aunt Beverly. "Don't say anything for a while, though, OK? Your

Dad and Grandpa Stone know, but I don't want the word to spread until I've got some more of the details nailed down."

"I won't," I said. "You know how I feel about nailing down details!" We both laughed. In some ways, it's scary how much I'm like Aunt Beverly.

Well, dear Journal, that just about brings you up to date. Thursday was a busy day. As if to confirm Aunt Beverly's idea about tourists, we had our *second* tourist bus stop at The Wonderful Life Shop. Once again, the people bought *lots* of things. The cash register seemed to be ringing up sales continually. Which reminded me. At the end of the day, as we were closing up the shop a half hour late—mainly because of the tourists—I mentioned to Aunt Beverly what Jon was doing at Stone's Hardware and how he and Dad had linked together the inventory computer program with the cash registers. "Jon was wondering if you'd need a system like that at the shop," I said.

"That's actually a very good idea," said Aunt Beverly. "I'd probably use it more as a marketing tool than an inventory program. Things don't seem to stay around long enough to become inventoried!" We both laughed. "Ask Jon if he can stop by some Saturday . . . he doesn't work on Saturdays, does he?"

"No," I said. "I'll ask him."

Thursday night we had our training ride.

About halfway through the ride, I came up with a thunderbolt idea—a true stroke of brilliance, if I do say so myself. It may be the best idea I've ever had . . . well, at least for this week. I can hardly wait to talk to Kimber and Trish about it tomorrow on the ride. There wasn't even any time to make a phone call today. Mrs. Miller and Dad and I went shopping for "major supplies," as Mrs. Miller said, immediately after I finished work. We went to Benton—Kiersti, too—and really stocked up on everything from a new vacuum cleaner to new bathroom rugs. Mrs. Miller has some major home improvements in mind! All in all, the house is feeling more like home all the time.

# Chapter Nine

# Lunch with
# Mrs. Webster

**Tuesday**
**8 P.M.**

*W*ell, dear Journal, we really pulled it off. The coup of the century . . . well, at least of this month in Collinsville.

On Saturday while we were riding our bikes, I had a chance to ride alongside Kimber for a ways, and then alongside Trish. We've found that it's best on our bike trips to ride along two-by-two, with one person in the lead. We change leaders every little ways. That way, we can talk and have fun, but at the same time, stay on the shoulder of the road and clear of the traffic.

Kimber and Trish both thought my idea was truly brilliant, so when we got back, we ganged up on Libby and told her what we had in mind. She seemed skeptical, but agreeable.

My next stop was to talk with Dad about whether we could use the house for our "plan" on Monday afternoon. He gave his permission, as long as Mrs. Miller was also in agreement. I then called Mrs. Miller to tell her what we wanted to do, and she thought it was a great idea. She said she'd help in any way she could. I told her I needed for her to be Trish's grandmother that day, and asked her if she could bring clothes she might change into. She agreed and seemed genuinely pleased to be included.

By that time, I was getting more and more excited, and feeling more and more confident! No sooner had I hung up the phone from talking to Mrs. Miller than Kimber called to say that her mom was willing to participate—Monday is her mother's day off at the clinic, which was part of our reason for choosing Monday as the day for our plan.

Next I called Aunt Beverly. I knew it was late, but I felt certain she'd still be up. As it turned out, she wasn't home! I later discovered that my suspicions were correct: She had been out with Mr. Clark Weaver!

On Sunday after church I finally got hold of Aunt Beverly. "And how was this date?" I said, guessing at where she had been Saturday night.

"Are you and Jon comparing notes about our

dating schedule?" she asked with a tease in her voice.

"No, I'm just winging a guess," I said.

"Well, you were lucky this time," she said. "We had a good time."

"Good?" I said. "That's such a boring nondescript word, Aunt Beverly!"

"I guess I'll just have to be your boring nondescript aunt, then," she laughed. Aunt Beverly is *anything* but boring or nondescript. Changing the subject, she asked, "What is the *real* reason for your call, my sweet niece?"

I told her what I had in mind and she not only agreed to come help me with my plan, but to come early and help me fix the food and set the table.

So, it was all set. Except, of course, that I needed to phone Mrs. Webster. I fussed and fumed about that for a little bit, but I finally got up my nerve about three o'clock to call and extend *the* invitation . . .

To a mother-daughter luncheon!

The way I figured it, Mrs. Webster needed to see that Libby has some very nice friends—true young ladies. I think I figured right!

Kimber had told her mother just a little bit about my conversation with Libby, and I had told Mrs. Miller just a little about it—and of course, I told it all to Aunt Beverly in word-by-word detail. So the other "mothers" had a little forewarning about the problem at hand, and the real reason behind the luncheon.

We all dressed in our Sunday finest. Kimber wore a beautiful pale pink sheath and had her hair pulled back in a chignon with a pink bow. She looked like she was sixteen, at least! Libby wore a two-piece pale lavender dress. It was new, as far as we all were concerned. Trish really surprised me by showing up in a dress. I'd never seen her in anything but jeans shorts or a jeans skirt and T-shirts. Granted, it was a T-shirt dress, but it was really cute and the perfect shade of blue for her. She had on big blue and crystal earrings that dressed up the whole look, and white high-heeled sandals instead of her usual canvas shoes. (Kimber admitted to me later that the shoes and earrings were actually hers.)

I wore a two-piece beige linen dress with eyelet at the waistline and hemline. I've had this dress for a year or so, but I keep forgetting to wear it here in Collinsville. It's the dress Aunt Beverly bought me for my fourteenth birthday last September.

On Monday morning, it hit me that I hadn't factored in Kiersten and Mari. They were delighted to be included and when I looked at them across the table from me, I was truly glad I hadn't forgotten them completely. Kiersten had on a pale green and white cotton dress with huge ruffles at the sleeveless armholes (the ruffles are so big they almost form sleeves), another Aunt Beverly find. Mari had on a blue and white striped dress with a white eyelet pinafore. They looked like dolls, even though I'm sure they would have thought that was too much of a little-girl description. I told them that they looked "superior" and they both beamed.

Aunt Beverly helped me with the food and setting the table, just as she had promised. We used all the best china and crystal.

Early Monday morning, I went shopping with Mrs. Miller and we got all the ingredients for what we needed. Aunt Beverly had said that she would bring dessert, and what a dessert she brought. It was a fabulous chocolate cheesecake!

Mrs. Miller and I worked for a couple of hours on lunch. She made cold cucumber soup—a soup I hated when I was a little girl, but which I now love. Funny how your taste buds change as you get older. (That's a Gramma Weber line.) We made finger sandwiches from fake crabmeat and chopped-up celery, egg, and mayonnaise. And then we made a salad and tossed it with giant croutons and cherry tomatoes and honey-mustard salad dressing.

If I do say so myself, everything turned out great. Aunt Beverly, of course, helped plan the menu. She also brought fresh flowers for the table,

**120**

and for the vases in the living room. Our house looked like something in a magazine by the time she finished the flowers and plumped all the pillows and rearranged a few of the magazines on the coffee table.

Everybody showed up at noon, just as expected. Mrs. Webster was quite impressed. I could tell that right away. It was all I could do to keep from shouting "Yes!"

The luncheon turned out to be a good idea on lots of different fronts. This was the first time that Aunt Beverly and Mrs. Chan had a good chance to talk. The same for Mrs. Chan and Mrs. Miller. Mrs. Webster, of course, had never met any of the women and none of us girls.

Mrs. Chan and Aunt Beverly had a little side conversation—which I just happened to overhear because I was sitting closest to them both—about the possibility of having a summer theater in Collinsville. What a fabulous idea! I can hardly wait to see if that develops. It could be just the nighttime entertainment that Collinsville needs to attract tourists. But I'm sure that's what Aunt Beverly already has in mind.

During the course of the luncheon, the conversation went just as I had hoped it would.

At one point, Mrs. Webster said, "I didn't know Libby had made such fine friends in Collinsville. She's always been so shy."

"Why, she and Kimber became friends just like that," said Mrs. Chan.

Mrs. Miller joined the chorus, as if right on cue, "She was one of the first friends Trish made. They seem to have a great time coming up with various ideas and projects."

"Your daughter is one of the most creative young ladies I know," added Aunt Beverly. "She and Trish composed a birthday song for one of their friends that was a genuine hoot!"

Mrs. Webster just beamed, although I'm not sure she knew what Aunt Beverly meant by "hoot." That's definitely an Aunt Beverly word. Libby looked a little embarrassed. I still don't think she thought this whole idea was going to work.

Then, as dessert was being served, Mrs. Chan said in her most refined voice, "Aren't you proud, Lillian, of the community service that these girls are performing?" (Lillian, by the way, is Mrs. Webster's first name.)

"I'm not sure I know what you mean," said Mrs. Webster. She looked a little panicky at that point, as if she had been left out of a secret. Which, of course, was precisely the point. If she talked to Libby more, she'd know what the FF Club is all about!

"Why the FF Club these girls have formed," said Aunt Beverly, picking right up where Mrs. Chan had left off. "The girls, and three of their other friends, have formed a club to provide community service. They have formed something of a litter patrol, and believe me, all of us in the Chamber of Commerce deeply appreciate what they are doing. Apart from keeping our city more beautiful, we think they're an excellent example to other young people in town."

Mrs. Webster looked at Libby as if she had discovered that her daughter might have some heretofore unseen value.

Mrs. Chan continued the praise, "I thought Kimber's bike-riding days were over, but I was sure wrong. She's put more miles on her bicycle in the past couple of weeks than in the last several years."

"Her bicycle?" asked Mrs. Webster, trying to put all the pieces together and still sound as if she knew exactly what was going on.

"Sure. That's what the FF Club does—they ride their bikes from toxic dump site to toxic dump site."

"Toxic dumps?" asked Mrs. Webster, now sounding a little alarmed.

"Oh, that was Libby's very creative way of describing major patches of litter," said Aunt Beverly as she leaned over to give Libby a hug and a big smile. "Your daughter has a real way with words."

"Well," said Mrs. Webster, "I'm pleased to hear all this . . . and I'm very glad to know that this club has such strong support from you other mothers. We can't be too careful about what our young people are involved in."

Mrs. Webster was *more* than just pleased, dear Journal, let me quickly assure you of that. She was just trying to sound sophisticated. I could tell Mrs. Webster was *bursting* with pride that her daughter was part of such an elite group of young ladies, who came from such fine families, and who were about such a noble cause!

It's a good thing she didn't see us later. Monday evening, we (Kimber, Trish, Libby, and I) met at Kimber's house and laughed at all that had happened, and especially at ourselves. There we were, in our grungies, giving each other high-fives over the luncheon's success—a far cry from the prim and proper "young ladies" who had charmed Mrs. Webster. (We went from being *Little Women* to *Jo's Boys* in the same day! Both of those books by Louisa May Alcott are among my favorites, by the way.)

"Mother said she was glad I had made such l-l-l-ladylike friends," said Libby, "and that she was glad she knew the full s-s-s-story about my bike riding. She implied, of course, that I hadn't t-t-t-told her the full s-s-s-story, but that's OK. I'm just glad she's going to let me r-r-r-ride."

"Me, too!" said Trish.

"Me, three!" said Kimber.

"Me, four!" I said.

Mrs. Chan came in and said, "You girls certainly gave Mrs. Webster a hard time. She didn't know whether to be surprised or pleased. I'm glad she didn't walk out on us."

"Well, you helped, Mom," said Kimber.

"And I'm glad I could," said Mrs. Chan, leaning over to give both Kimber and Libby a hug at the same time. "Sometimes we mothers just don't see how wonderful our own daughters are."

I couldn't help but notice that Trish became very quiet when Mrs. Chan said that. She was pretty quiet for the rest of the evening. I think she must really be missing her mom. Funny, though. She never talks about her parents. Maybe we just haven't had much time lately for serious conversations.

## Chapter Ten

# Two Incidents on Highway 9

*A*s the old saying goes, "There's good news and there's bad news." Both of which happened yesterday evening on our last practice ride.

I've been eager all day to get home to you, dear Journal, to tell you all about the evening. And now that I'm here, with pen in hand, I hardly know where to begin.

Perhaps I should start with the bad news first. Linda and Ford Milner—you remember the two kids that Jon met in the hardware store when he sold them a birdbath for their mom?—well, they *did* decide to become a part of the FF Club, and last Tuesday, they joined us for our first bike ride. I realize I forgot to tell you about all that. Jon mentioned them at the next meeting after he had met them and everybody said it sounded great to have them join us, so Jon called them. They said they'd been thinking about it and that the club sounded like fun to both of them, but that they were going on vacation with their family for ten days, so they'd join us when they got back. Jon got their T-shirt sizes so we had T-shirts ready for them on Tuesday, which was the first day they could ride with us.

Anyway, they really fit right into the club. It was like they'd been friends with us from the start. Ford is fifteen but really tall for his age. In fact, he's taller than anyone else in the club. He's very shy, but he's also polite and when he does talk, he seems very nice. Linda, on the other hand, is a chatterbox and just about the opposite from her brother in every way. She's short and pretty "plump," as Gramma Weber would say—compared to Ford being so tall and thin. She also has dark hair, compared to Ford's blond hair. And she's very outgoing. We all really took to her right away, and fortunately for us, she didn't mind hanging around with a group of fourteen- and fifteen-year-olds, even though she's sixteen. (It helps that Dennis is also sixteen, although I noticed that Kimber stuck extra close to Dennis when she found out that Linda is sixteen.)

We were on our route down toward River Gorge when tragedy struck. We'd all dismounted from our bicycles to tackle an especially bad "toxic dump" when Linda asked, "Where do you all go to church?"

Dennis and Julio said the Baptist church and the rest of us said Faith Community Fellowship.

"Oh," said Linda, very innocently and brightly, "do you know our cousins? Their last name is Wilson, and they go to Faith Community Fellowship."

"Tad Wilson?" asked Trish, who immediately was all ears.

"Right," said Linda. "I'm glad you know them. They're really neat people. I hope you don't mind my saying that about my aunt and uncle and cousins."

"Not at all," said Trish. "We think they're neat, too. We were at a swim party at their house."

"Isn't that a great old house?" said Linda. "It was my grandparents' house, and after they both died, Uncle Marv and Aunt Louise moved into it. We don't see them very much since we moved. But when we were little, Ford and I spent almost every day playing with Tad and Cindy."

"Cindy?" said Trish. "I thought Tad's sister was named Alice."

"Oh, she is," said Linda. "Boy, was that a slip of the tongue! I must have said 'Cindy' because we just saw Tad and Cindy last Saturday over at Castle Rock."

"Were you at Castle Rock?" I asked. "I used to live at Eagle Point."

"Did you?" said Linda. "We have a vacation house at Castle Rock, but for years, we rented a little house in Eagle Point during the summers. It was on Bay View Street, right above the theater and Benny's Ice Cream Parlor."

"I know exactly where that is," I said. "We lived up on Crest."

"Now that's a view," said Linda.

"Who's Cindy?" asked Trish, changing the subject back to what was really important to her.

"Oh, Cindy is Tad's girlfriend," said Linda. And there you have it, a major bombshell.

I couldn't see Trish's face because her back was to me, but I saw her shoulders stiffen as if she had been hit in the stomach.

"We didn't meet her at the swim party," I said, hoping to ease the tension that I suddenly felt in the air.

"She probably was working that night. She works on weekends at the Collinsville Club. Her parents aren't too happy about her working on Sundays, and neither is Tad, but it doesn't seem to bother her."

"Is she a Christian?" I asked.

"I *think* so," said Linda. "As far as I know, she was going with Tad to Faith Community Fellowship before she started her job—which was, oh, about Easter time, I guess."

"That explains it," I said. "I just moved to Collinsville last spring, right after Easter."

"Are they serious?" asked Trish. Linda doesn't know Trish well enough to know that her voice sounded really shaky and weak when she asked that question.

"Yeah, I'd say so," said Linda. "They've been dating since before Christmas, and they've both made plans to go to the same college in September."

"Where are they going?" I asked, trying to keep the conversation going so Trish wouldn't get stuck if Linda ever thought to ask, "Why do you ask?" Fortunately, Linda didn't seem to be aware that anything was going on.

"McKinney College," said Linda. "Have you ever heard of it?"

"Heard of it?" I said. "It's where I plan to go someday. My mother and Aunt Beverly both graduated from McKinney College."

"Really?" said Linda. "Small world. I'd never heard of it until Tad told me that he and Cindy are going there."

By this time, Trish had drifted away toward Dennis and Julio in picking up litter. I tied the sack that Linda and I had finished filling and set it by the side of the road. We had decided that if

**130**

we filled sacks completely, we'd set them by the road and come back later and pick them up in Grandpa Stone's pickup. (That's part of what Grandpa Stone offered when he gave us the T-shirts and baseball caps.)

I could tell Trish was really upset inside, but she managed to hide it well. Dennis and Julio didn't seem to notice that her laughter was a little bit forced or that she was talking a little louder than usual . . . but I noticed. I wanted to go to her and put my arms around her and let her cry, but I'm really not sure why I felt that way. In the first place, I'm not sure Trish would have cried, or even have let me touch her. She's pretty distant in things like that. Still, my heart went out to her.

"What's up?" said Jon, interrupting my thoughts of the moment.

"Nothing," I said.

"You look like you just lost your best friend," he said, and then pointing at himself, he added with a grin, "but I'm h-e-r-e."

"So you are!" I said, laughing. "And I'm glad. I'm also glad for the rakes that Grandpa Stone suggested we take along today. He must have known things were bad over in this area." Looking around at the five or six piles of trash we'd raked together on the otherwise clean stretch of road we'd just created, I said, "Do you think we've worked enough of a miracle here?"

"I'd say so," he said. "There's another bad patch just around the bend. I've already scouted it out and I think I'll go down there and start working while everybody sacks up these piles."

"Good idea," I said, handing him my rake.

And that, dear Journal, is how the second incident on Highway 9 happened to be set up.

About ten minutes or so after Jon had left, we finished sacking up all the trash and headed off toward the direction Jon had gone. Between where Jon was, though, and where we had been, is a little gas station. We all decided it was a good idea to stop there. Julio put air in Kimber's front tire. A few of us went to the rest rooms and a couple of others got things out of the vending machines. We were pretty inconspicuous (don't you just love that word?) by the side of the road, kinda scattered out among the cars and people at the gas station. That's probably why The Four Creeps didn't pay much attention to us as they went zooming by.

I heard the sound of their car even before I saw it. Their car must have a bad muffler or something. Anyway, the car has a very distinct sound. I stopped dead in my tracks when I heard it, and I said to Dennis, who was standing closest to me, "That's the sound of trouble coming."

"What?" he said.

"Yes, it's definitely trouble," I said as the old blue car with the white top and giant tailfins slith-

**132**

ered around the corner, squealing a little as it did.

"That guy's got muffler and tire trouble, if that's what you mean," said Dennis.

Suddenly, all I could think about was Jon working alone down the road a few hundred yards.

"That's not what I mean," I said. "I mean *real* trouble for Jon. We've got to hurry."

Dennis seemed alarmed at the sound of my voice, and I probably did sound pretty hysterical as I got on my bike and began peddling away as fast as I could after the blue car with the squealing tires.

He hurriedly called to all of the other FF clubbers and within seconds, they were all on their bicycles trailing behind me. Julio caught up with me at the first bend in the winding road.

"What's the panic?" he shouted at me.

"Those guys have it in for Jon and he's all alone!" By that time, Dennis had come up close enough to hear what was going on. He and Julio sped on ahead of me a little.

Jon told me later what happened from his perspective. He had raked together a couple of small piles of trash at the wide place in the road just above the River Gorge Café when he, too, had heard the sound of the car coming down the hill. He said, "I knew right away who it was. I didn't even have to think about it. Must have been instinct. Anyway, I moved as far away from the edge

**133**

of the road as I could in hopes those guys wouldn't see me . . . but no such luck. They spotted me, and a few yards down the road, I heard Dirk slam on his brakes. I knew the road was too narrow for them to turn around right there, but that it was only a matter of a couple minutes before they got to the entrance of the River Gorge Café, where it would be easy for them to turn around."

"What did you think?" I asked him.

"Dozens of things," said Jon. "My mind was racing. In the first place, I became very aware of the rock ledge that was behind me and along the edge of the road where I was working. Although the shoulder was extra wide there, like a turn-out spot, I was also totally blocked off from any escape if they pinned me against that wall. I thought about crossing the road and running into the wooded area toward the river, but I knew that I'd have to leave my bike behind, and I figured that if they couldn't find me, they'd probably destroy my bicycle."

"Not a good option," I said.

"I knew that I couldn't make it back up the hill to the gas station before they had turned around, and that if I was partway there, there was a good chance I could become a hit-and-run victim. I wasn't wild about the idea of you all finding *me* as trash by the side of the road," said Jon, with a wry grin.

**134**

"Definitely not a good option," I said.

"S-o-o-o-o . . . ," he drawled, "I had just about decided that the best thing for me to do was to wait until they were almost back to where I was, and to race off *toward* them."

"Toward them?" I asked. "Wouldn't that have put you right in their path?"

"Well, I was hoping that they wouldn't have a fast enough reaction time to swerve and pin me against the rock wall, and by speeding past them toward the café, I hoped I'd make it to the café in the time it took them to turn around and come after me. It would have been cutting it close, though."

"I'm glad you didn't try that," I said. "They could have run you off the road into the woods toward the river."

"That thought also occurred to me," said Jon. "Like I said . . . my mind was racing. Which is why I did nothing, I guess. My mind was moving, but my feet weren't. I had just remounted my bike when I saw them come around the bend. That was about two seconds past the point that I had intended to speed away, and it was just long enough for them to block that side of the road and skid into the turn-out where I was standing. A truck came by so I couldn't cross the road and ride away on that side of them. I was, in a word, *stuck.*"

"I never would have been able to think *or*

move," I said. "I know I would have panicked and been like a stone."

"That's pretty much the way I felt when the guys pulled up and I saw that my only exit had been blocked by that truck. The guys jumped out of the car and all came toward me, saying things I'd rather not repeat."

"What did they say?" I demanded.

"Oh, you don't need to know," said Jon. "They used a lot of swear words and called me a bunch of names.

"All I had with me was the rake and the litter spear that I was holding in one hand. I knew that the litter spear, with that little nail on the end, would be my best weapon, but I also knew that two of them could easily pull that away from me and use it against me. I decided to just hold my ground and see what would happen. I figured it would be harder for them to hit me if I was on my bike than if I was off it, and that a few of their blows might hit metal instead of me."

"And then the cavalry showed up!" I said excitedly.

"Exactly," said Jon. "You guys were the best sight these old eyes of mine could possibly have seen."

"I was really afraid we'd be too late," I said.

"No, the timing was perfect," said Jon. "First, Dennis and Julio rounded the bend, both of them shouting at the top of their lungs. It was like they had their swords drawn and a battle cry going. Julio had his rake over his head and Dennis was holding out his litter spear as if he was in a jousting match. They skidded to a stop in the roadway about fifteen feet from me. I looked back quickly to see the surprise on the faces of Dirk, Jim, Paul, and Skip. They quickly looked at each other and I could tell they were sizing up the situation fast. So far, it was only three against four, even if the three had a couple of sticks. They took a step toward me—"

"And that's when the rest of us showed up!"

"Exactly," said Jon.

"We had heard Dennis and Julio holler, so we started hollering, too," I said.

"Do you remember that story in the Bible, in 2 Kings 7, about how the Lord made four crippled lepers sound like a whole army to the enemy that was encamped outside the city walls?"

"Yes," I said. "We studied that in Sunday school in Eagle Point right before I moved to Collinsville!"

"Well, that must have been what happened," Jon said. "Those guys looked at each other again and reached an entirely different decision. By the time you and Ford rounded the bend with your rakes and litter spears in your hands, they were already moving back toward their car."

"They were just turning around when we pulled to a stop by Dennis and Julio," I said.

"Right, and they got in their car when they saw Trish, Kimber, Linda, and Libby round the bend," said Jon. "You know, with your bike helmets on, it's not all that easy to tell from a distance that you girls are *girls*."

"It's a good thing they weren't yelling," I laughed. "Their high-pitched voices might have given them away."

"By that time, it was nine against four—and not only that, but nine 'armed' riders—and those geeks knew they were outnumbered. They got in their car, made a couple of rude gestures, and roared away."

"Best roar I've ever heard," I said.

Jon grinned. "As they got into their car, I couldn't help but yell, 'Does this mean you don't want to join us?'" He laughed a little and then went on, "You should have seen how you guys all looked. There you were, all standing with your bicycles, rakes and litter spears by your sides, like Indian warriors with their spears on the top of a cliff. Heap big power!"

I laughed. "To the rescue!" I said loudly. "And then you said, 'I take it you *don't* want them to be members of our club?'"

"I just had to say *something*," said Jon, "to get over being so *scared*."

**138**

"Can you imagine Dirk, Jim, Paul, and Skip ever wanting to be members of the FF Club?" I asked.

Jon got very serious. "Not unless they wanted to destroy it."

"Oh, don't even say that," I said. "Bad idea. Forget I ever said anything about it."

"By the way," Jon said, switching gears. "What was it that Dennis and Julio, and then you and Ford, were shouting as they rounded the bend?"

"Friends!" I said. "We were shouting *Fr-ie-ie-ie-ie-ie-ie-nds!*"

"I could only make out the '*eh*' sound," said Jon. "That's great. Friends! Pretty good battle cry."

"It's the best," I said. Jon grinned.

I can't tell you, dear Journal, how relieved I was that Jon was safe. I'm hoping our show of strength for Jon means that those guys never, ever, ever come back. At least that's my prayer.

After we cleaned up that patch of litter—which we did in record time, I might add—we rode on down to River Gorge Café. I called Grandpa Stone from there and he came to pick us up with his truck. Winding our way back up the road we gathered the trash bags. I think we all had one ear listening for the squeal of an old blue and white Pontiac, but The Four Creeps didn't show their faces again.

On the ride back, Linda asked, "Are your club meetings and bike rides always this exciting?"

"I hope not!" I said.

And I especially hope, dear Journal, that we have no such incidents tomorrow when we make our big trek to Benton. I'm hoping, too, that I get a chance to talk to Trish while we ride.

# Chapter Eleven

# Benton
or Bust!

**Saturday**
**9 P.M.**

*W*ell, we made it!

Thirty-five miles, fifteen sacks of litter, and lots of sunscreen later! Actually, it took us nearly twelve hours to make the ride. It wasn't all that bad, even though there *was* more litter than we had counted on.

About halfway through the morning, Libby came up with the line that pretty much summed up our feelings about the day and the litter. She moaned, "What ever happened to 'Keep America B-b-b-beautiful'?" We were all wondering the same thing.

In the end, that's the line that Jon used when he was interviewed by the television cameras. But . . . I'm getting ahead of myself.

We left Jon's house at six in the morning, deciding that it was definitely to our advantage to get an early start and avoid the heat. We had originally thought we'd make it to Benton by noon, but within a couple of hours, it became very evident that we weren't going to make that goal—not by a long shot.

It's only four miles from Collinsville to the Highway 142 intersection—out past the Collinsville Club. It's really a pretty ride—lots of trees line one side of the two-lane road, and once you are past the club, the orchards and vegetable farms appear. So did several major trash areas.

Fortunately, we had brought tons of food, so we stopped about 8:30 and had breakfast in the little park that's just off the road where Highway 9 turns into Highway 142.

The worst trash was between that intersection and the intersection between Highway 142 and Highway 139, which is the main road that goes between Benton and Fruitvale, and on over to Eagle Point. It's only an eight-mile stretch, but it took us four hours to ride, and "litter sweep"—which is Trish's term.

Speaking of Trish, I had a chance to talk to her a little bit.

"I hope you aren't too upset about Tad," I said.

"What's to be upset about?" she said, with a real chip on her shoulder. "He's got a girlfriend."

"I know, but . . ." I couldn't seem to find the right words.

"Actually," said Trish, sounding more like her old self, "I never even got a chance to make an impression! If he had ever met the real me . . . 'bye, 'bye, Cindy."

"That's right!" I said. "She wouldn't have had a chance."

I knew Trish was covering up, and she probably knew that I knew, but that's where we left it.

When we got to the intersection between highways 142 and 139, we pulled over and had lunch at the McDonald's there. We decided we might want the rest of our sandwiches and snacks in a couple of hours. It felt like we were rationing out supplies! After all, we had been on the road for seven and a half hours by that time, and we had only gone twelve miles. We still had twenty-three miles to go.

We had a few minutes' discussion about whether we should call it a day and not go on to Benton, but we decided to press on. We weren't all that tired—from either the riding or the trash. And it wasn't as hot as we had thought it might be. We just weren't making very good time. So we filled our water bottles and pressed on.

Conditions along Highway 139 were *far* better. There was hardly any trash, so mostly we concentrated on our riding.

Highway 139 is a four-laner. In our practice rides, we had only been on one four-laner before—a wide avenue out toward East Valley—but that had only been for a few blocks. There, we had taken over one lane of the road, riding three abreast. That worked fine for battling in-town traffic, but out on the highway, things were different.

We quickly realized that the best thing for us to do was to ride single file, and fairly spaced out. We regrouped after about a half-mile at a turn-out spot and decided that we'd just try to spear litter as we rode along. If the first person missed, then the next person might get the litter, and so forth. We realized in deciding to take that approach that we might miss a few pieces. If we really encountered a toxic waste dump, we decided the first rider would hold up his litter spear and rake, and we'd all plan to stop.

Our final decision was probably the best one. We decided that a slow rider should lead the pack. Which meant one of us girls. We knew that if a guy led, by the time we got to the last rider, we'd be stretched out over several miles. Libby and Linda looked at each other and said, "They mean one of us!" We all laughed, but it was true. So . . . Linda and Libby took turns leading and they had a fun time with their shared role as leader.

In all, we only encountered two toxic dump sites that required us to stop in the twenty-three-mile stretch of Highway 139. We filled up a couple of bags at each and left them there.

We stopped at about 3:30 in the afternoon and finished off the peanut-butter sandwiches, chips, and apples. (The chicken and tuna sandwiches had all been eaten at breakfast.) We stopped at a weigh station to fill up our water bottles about a mile after lunch, so we had plenty of water for the rest of the ride.

And . . . we pulled into Benton at 6:13 in the evening. We had each made guesses before we started as to the exact minute of our arrival, and Kimber won by a landslide with her guess of 2:10. *Nobody* had thought it would take us as long as it did to reach the first Burger King on the outskirts of Benton. I think because it took so long, we were extra proud of ourselves.

We also hadn't counted on being greeted by reporters and cameramen from all three TV stations in Benton, reporters from both the *Benton Gazette* and the *Collinsville Herald*, the mayor of Collinsville, and Miss Jones, the head of the Collinsville Chamber of Commerce!

Aunt Beverly, Dad, Grandpa Stone, Dr. Chan, and Mr. Clark Weaver were also there. So were Kiersten and Mari. It was a real welcoming committee! We had been so intent on our work, that we hadn't even seen the cars from Collinsville pass. Aunt Beverly admitted to me that she had called the press. "It's a *good* story, and we need more of those," she whispered to me when I asked her if all the hoopla was her idea.

As president of the FF Club, I had to make a statement to all the cameras and reporters about how we started the club and what we hoped to do—to combine fun and community service. Jon was interviewed, too, as vice-president. He talked about how we came up with the bike-ride idea (modestly not telling them that it was *his* idea, I noticed), and decided to combine it with a litter sweep.

And then the mayor gave us a special award, recognizing us as an "official" community-service club in Collinsville. That means we'll get to hang a shield on the club board at the entrance to the city, right along with the Lions, Kiwanis, and Rotary clubs! We had never even thought of *that!*

To top it all off, Miss Jones announced to the media that Jon, Libby, and I are to be named to a new youth advisory board for the Bridge-to-Benton committee that the Chamber of Commerce is forming. I don't know much about that committee, but it sounds pretty important . . . so we were excited.

And that still isn't all. Grandpa Stone surprised us by taking the entire group to the Lazy J Family Steakhouse for dinner. "I thought I was going to get away with a Burger King lunch," he said with a laugh, "but you kids did too good a job cleaning up the roadways!"

The Lazy J is a very casual place, but they really do have the biggest salad bar in the world . . . well, at least the biggest I've seen in Benton . . . and they have great steaks. Grandpa Stone said the expense was well worth it. "Where else can I buy such cheap advertising for Stone's Hardware?" he said, tugging at my baseball cap even as he spoke.

"But, Grandpa," I reminded him, "we were mostly wearing our bicycle helmets when we were interviewed. You should have reminded me to put on my cap before I talked to the reporters. We didn't put on our caps until later."

"That's why I positioned the cameras so you'd be standing in front of my Stone's Hardware truck," he said with a little chuckle. Grandpa is always thinking!

We kids climbed into the back of Grandpa's pickup and stashed most of our bikes in the back of the Weaver and Chan vans for the trip home. We sang all the way back to Collinsville, full stomachs and all. Some fun songs—like the kind we all sang when we went to camp as kids—and a few of the faster choruses we sing at Faith Community Fellowship.

We were only able to pick up five of the litter bags on the way home, so after we got to Collinsville and unloaded everything, Grandpa Stone, Dad, Jon, and Mr. Clark Weaver went back along the route we had taken and picked up the other ten bags. By the time they swung by the dumpster behind the store, they didn't get home until about 10:30.

It was a really full day, as you can tell. I literally collapsed into bed. But not before Kiersti gave me a big hug and said, "I'm so proud of you, Katelyn." She really is a doll at times.

# Chapter Twelve

# Turning Points

*W*hat a day *this* has been! By day, I probably mean the last twenty-four hours, not just Monday.

The first exciting thing that happened was a talk I had right after youth group. Dennis dropped Jon and me both off at my house and Jon said, "Are you tired after the ride yesterday?"

"Not really," I said. "It was too much fun to be tiring."

"I agree," he said. "I had a good chance to talk to Ford on Saturday."

"Oh?" I said. "He seems really shy. I don't feel as if I know him very well yet, but what I know, I like."

"He's a great guy," said Jon. "I'm going over to his house tomorrow night to try out a couple of computer programs he has."

"He's into computers?" I asked.

"Yeah," said Jon, "he's a nerd just like me."

"Well," I said, "in my opinion, neither one of you are nerds. Computers are *in*, Jon, or hadn't you noticed that we're getting closer to the twenty-first century all the time?"

"I noticed," he said, grinning. "Ford has lots of game programs. I've never really fooled around with very many games. I'm looking forward to seeing what they're like."

"Sounds like fun."

"I just might have an idea for our next project as the FF Club," said Jon.

"What is it?" I said. "Your last one was sure great."

"I'll tell you when I have it more focused," said Jon, who then quickly changed the subject by adding, "Ford also likes to play golf."

"Great," I said. "Sounds as if you two have a lot in common."

"Yeah," said Jon, "I think we do. It's nice to find someone that sorta speaks my language. Dennis and Julio are great friends, but I'm not really good at the things they like to do, and they aren't good at what I enjoy. We're learning, but with Ford, it's like we're right in sync."

As Jon said good night and walked home, I felt really excited for him. He's finally found a *real* friend in Collinsville—and maybe Ford can convince him that he doesn't need to change who he is on the inside in order to be popular. I don't want Jon to change *anything* about the way he is.

No sooner had Jon left than the phone rang and it was Kimber—who had truly exciting news to share!

"He kissed me," she said quietly, not even bothering to tell me who was calling, or to give me any build-up at all.

"He *did?*" I nearly shouted into the phone.

"Yes!" said Kimber, shouting back into the phone and laughing at the same time.

"Was it wonderful?" I asked.

"Truly," she said.

"Well, tell me what happened," I said. "All the details. Start at the beginning."

"There's really not all that much to tell," she said. "Dennis dropped off you and Jon and then instead of turning toward my house, he headed for Libby's house. He dropped her off and when we got back to my house, I started to get out of the car, but he held my arm back as I turned to get out. When I turned around to see what he wanted, he reached over with his other hand and turned my head toward him, and then he just leaned over and kissed me."

"Did he say anything?" I asked. I wished I were there in person with her. I knew I wasn't doing the living room sofa any good by jumping up and down on it—half seated and half on my knees— and crunching up the pillows.

"Not really," Kimber said. "After he kissed me, he just said, 'Good night, Kimber.' And that was all. I got out of the car and went to the house."

"Was it a long kiss?" I asked. "Details, Kimber. I want d-e-e-e-e-tails."

"No. It was just short and nice. I could tell that he kinda wanted to kiss me again, but when he said, 'Good night, Kimber,' I said, 'Good night, Dennis,' and that pretty much broke the spell. He had such a wonderful look in his eyes, though, Katelyn. I thought I was going to melt right then and there."

"Oh, this is so exciting," I said. "Did you tell your mom?"

"I didn't get a chance," said Kimber. "She came around the corner into the hall just as I walked in and closed the door. I guess I must have been leaning back against the door with a dreamy look on my face or something, because she just looked at me and said, 'I hope he wipes the lipstick off his face before he goes into *his* house!'"

"How did she know?" I asked, still not doing the sofa any favors.

"I looked in the mirror and my lipstick *was* a bit smeared," Kimber said. "That and the look on my face probably gave me away. Mom wasn't mad, though. She had a big smile on her face. And I don't think Dennis saw that my lipstick was a little goofy."

"I'm sure he didn't," I said. "Not if he was looking in your eyes."

We talked for a few more minutes, and then I went to bed. I couldn't sleep for a while though. I was too excited for Kimber. I couldn't help but think, *I wonder what it would be like . . .*

So much for romance. The news of this morning was anything but romantic.

Mrs. Miller walked into our house about eight o'clock. Dad and Kiersten and I were still at the breakfast table. Monday is my day off so I was still in my nightgown. So was Kiersti. "Have you heard from Trish?" she said, a very frantic tone to her voice.

"No," I said. "What's happened?"

"Well," said Mrs. Miller, "when I looked into her room this morning on my way out to work, I discovered that she wasn't there—only a big lump of T-shirts in her bed. I called to her, but there was no answer. When I got to the garage, I saw that her bicycle was gone. I thought maybe you had a special ride planned for this morning, so I just hurried on over here. Oh dear, I suspect there's more to this than I had thought."

"I'm sure it's nothing," I said, but in my heart I just knew that wasn't the case.

"Did she say anything about any plans that she had today?" asked Mrs. Miller.

"No," I said. "I talked to her yesterday afternoon to see if she was going to come to youth group with us, but she said that she had something else she needed to do and to tell everybody 'hi' for her. She sounded normal."

"Well," said Mrs. Miller. "This isn't like her at all. In the first place, she hardly ever gets up before I leave, and her job at Tony's doesn't start until eleven o'clock. Whenever she goes anywhere, she nearly always leaves me a little note on the kitchen counter."

"Let's call Tony's," Dad suggested. "Maybe he needed her to come in early today for some reason." Trish got a summer job working at Tony's Pizza Parlor during the lunch hour. She's really seemed to enjoy her job there, and has made some good money in tips.

Dad phoned but we could tell just a couple moments into the phone conversation that Trish wasn't there.

"Tony said that last Friday, Trish had asked to take this coming week off. He said that she'd arranged for a girl named Libby to come in and work for her."

"Libby?" I said. "Libby didn't say anything about that." I immediately reached for the phone and called Libby. "Are you working at Tony's this week?"

"Yeah," said Libby when she finally woke up enough to understand what I was saying. "Didn't I tell you that? Trish said she was going on vacation with her g-g-g-grandma this week and she asked if I could fill in for her. I worked at a p-p-p-pizza place before we moved to Collinsville so she knew I could handle the j-j-j-job. You really don't need to talk to the c-c-c-customers much. Why?"

"Well," I said, "I'm sitting here staring at Trish's grandma, that's why. They aren't going on any vacation this week, and Trish has disappeared!"

"Oh no!" said Libby. "Where do you think she's g-g-g-gone?"

"I don't know," I said. "I'll call you later." Turning to Dad and Mrs. Miller, I said, "Libby doesn't know anything. She said that Trish told her that you two were going on a vacation this week."

"Oh, why would she tell a lie like that?" Mrs. Miller said, collapsing into one of the kitchen chairs in a heap. Kiersten jumped up and ran over and threw her arms around her. "It'll be OK," she said.

"Do you have any ideas, Katelyn? This could be serious," Dad said, pulling me aside a little so Mrs. Miller couldn't hear him.

"Well, one," I said. "When we got to Highway 139 on Saturday, I was riding next to Trish and she commented, 'This is the highway to Fruitvale.' I know she's been missing her mom lately. I think she may have tried to ride her bicycle home."

"But that's sixty miles," Dad said.

"I know," I said. "That's what Trish said. She mentioned that, too, on the ride. She said, 'Maybe we should plan our next long trip to Fruitvale. It would probably only take a day since we've cleaned up all the messy parts getting out to Highway 139.' I just laughed when she said that and said, 'And then the next week we could go all the way to Eagle Point.' I never dreamed she might be serious."

Mrs. Miller then asked us, "What do you think I should do? Should I phone the police?"

"Not yet," said Dad. "Kat and I are going to go out in the van and see if we can find her. Katelyn knows her favorite hangouts, you know."

I hurried and got dressed. Never mind the hair and makeup. I just scrunched my hair up under a baseball cap and put on dark glasses. I was ready in about two minutes . . . well, probably three.

Dad and I headed off down Highway 9 and then up 142. No luck. We made it all the way to Fruitvale, but didn't see Trish anywhere. Once in Fruitvale, Dad and I couldn't quite remember how to get to Trish's house. Nothing looked very familiar and we couldn't remember the street names. Finally, we drove to the other side of town and turned around, thinking that if we approached the city from the Eagle Point side, we might remember which turns we had taken. It worked! We finally got to Trish's house, but by this time it was nearly 11:30. There was no answer when we rang the bell. We noticed a couple of newspapers on the driveway.

"Doesn't look as if anybody is at home," said Dad.

"Worse than that," I said. "It looks like Trish's mom and dad may have gone on a little vacation themselves."

"That's not particularly good news."

"What should we do?" I asked.

"Well, at this point, we probably should drive back to Collinsville," Dad said. "First, let's call home and see if maybe Mrs. Miller has heard from Trish."

No such luck. Mrs. Miller sounded a little frantic. She hadn't heard from Trish, and Kiersten had started to worry because *she* hadn't heard from us. We assured her that we were still looking and that we'd be home in a little while. Dad didn't tell her we were in Fruitvale.

So . . . we drove back home along Highway 139, Highway 142, and Highway 9. Still no sign of Trish. We pulled into the driveway at home about 1:30 to find Jon and Kimber at the house with Mrs. Miller and Kiersten. They said Libby had been calling every fifteen minutes, and Julio and Dennis had volunteered to drive around town and look, too.

"Did Trish say anything to you?" I asked Jon, pulling him to one side.

"No," said Jon.

"Did she say anything to you about riding to Fruitvale?" I said, nearly in a whisper.

"No," said Jon, and then he added, "she did say, though, that she felt as if she could ride to Benton and *back*. She was feeling pretty strong."

"I think maybe she tried to ride home," I said. And no sooner had I said that, than I heard Mrs. Miller say, "Oh, honey, are you all right?"

Dad had apparently confessed to Mrs. Miller where we had been and she had gone to the telephone straight away and had called the home of Trish's parents. We were all hugging each other in the kitchen as we heard the rest of the conversation—even though it was just Mrs. Miller's side of the conversation that we could hear.

"No, I know they aren't there," said Mrs. Miller. "They took a little trip together . . . Yes, I hope it's good news, too. . . . How did you get in? . . . Of course, you have a key . . . I've been terribly worried . . . No, the lump you made in the bed *didn't* look like you . . . Will you stay there until I can come over and be with you? . . . Promise me? . . . I'm sure the Webers will let me have a little time off." With that she looked at Dad and Dad, of course, nodded a big "yes." "I'll be there in an hour or so, honey. Stay right there, OK? . . . Promise? . . . OK, I'll see you in a little bit."

With that, Mrs. Miller hung up the phone and burst into tears. "She's all right," she said.

"Are you sure you feel up to driving over there by yourself?" Dad asked. "If not, I can drive you over and—"

"Thank you," said Mrs. Miller, "but no. I can make it. That is, if it's all right with you that I take a couple of days off. I think Trish and I need to spend a little time together over in Fruitvale."

"Take all the time you need," said Dad. And with that, Mrs. Miller gave each one of us a big hug and left.

"Is Trish going to be OK?" asked Kiersten.

"We've got to believe that," said Dad. "She really loves her grandmother and that's a big plus."

I noticed that Jon still had his arm on my shoulder, but when Mrs. Miller drove away, he took it down and said, "Back to work. I just realized my father—who also happens to be my boss this afternoon—doesn't know where *I* am!"

Oh, dear Journal, my head is just spinning as I write all this. So much to think about, and here we are at the end of another book!

*Will Trish come back with Mrs. Miller?*

*Will things really become romantic between Dennis and Kimber?*

*What is Jon's idea for a new FF Club project? And what will it mean for Jon and Libby and me to be on the Bridge-to-Benton committee?*

*Will Aunt Beverly's idea for a menswear shop take off? What will happen between her and Mr. Clark Weaver?*

*Will Libby like working at Tony's? Will things improve between Libby and her mother?*

*Will I ever see the mystery girl again? It's been three weeks since I saw her, and yet I have thought of her every day!*

The summer is just beginning and there's already so much to think about!

For now, though, I must close—not only for the night, but for this book. And in my tradition of tying up loose ends, I'll have to say for now . . .

# The End

Katelyn Weber
June
Collinsville

An excerpt from *Summer of Choices*, book three in the Forever Friends series:

"You still like Mr. Clark Weaver, though, don't you, Aunt Beverly?"

"Sure," she said brightly. "Why wouldn't I?"

"Well, I thought maybe that business about the money . . ."

"Heavens, no," she said. "That's about the only uncomfortable moment I've had with Clark. He's a very easy person to be around. We've got lots of things in common, and it's really nice to spend some time with a guy who is a Christian."

"Sounds like dating to me," I said.

"Just friends," Aunt Beverly said.

"So when does 'just friends' become dating—given the fact that you go so many places together and do so much together?" I asked.

"Are you and Jon dating?" Aunt Beverly asked.

"No!" I said.

"But don't you spend a lot of time together and go places together?" she asked.

"Yes . . . but . . ."

"But what?" Aunt Beverly asked.

Watch for *Summer of Choices* at a bookstore near you.